CELESTIAL LAND AND SEA

AMY McLEAN

Published by Open Books

Cover image "The Ship" Copyright ©Mariusz

Learn more about the artist at
http://akpelan.deviantart.com/

ISBN: 0692389997
ISBN-13: 978-0692389997

DEDICATION

For Lynda and Robin.

1

*T*he earth crunched beneath the wheels as the carriage made its way through the iron gates. They'd returned later than intended, a delay caused by an unexpected downpour, but with no other engagements that evening she didn't consider it to be of any great concern. Perhaps, if she allowed herself to think about it, it might have actually been a blessing; the days were growing longer now, her mind becoming wearier as time seemed to crawl by.

The coachman pulled open the door to allow Elizabeth to step out. He'd steered the carriage as closely to the entrance as possible to save Her Majesty from the torrential weather, but no precaution could have prevented Elizabeth's hair from becoming soaked as she rushed inside the palace. Her outer garments were tended to as she shook the water from her face. She had to admit it felt good to be home after a tiring day.

"I wish to sup alone this evening."

"Yes, Your Majesty," came the reply before she retired to her bedchambers. Not that she ever believed she was truly on her own.

It's beautiful, isn't it? she thought to herself once she had arrived upstairs. She was watching the rain as it continued to wash down the sides of the building. It pelted the surface of the river, splashing into tiny whirlpools. The shower was coming down fast and hard, and it didn't offer any indication that it was going to stop any time soon.

"I suppose the city was in need of a good cleansing anyway," she mumbled as she gazed out the window, standing just outside the door to her bedchambers. She fought to erase the images of the countless infected bodies they'd passed on their journey back to the palace. How many had there been? It would have been impossible for her to count them, but she was certain numbers were increasing.

Not wishing to think about the disturbing conditions of London's streets any longer than she had to, she allowed her thoughts to drift back to the view in front of her. The long corridor that overlooked the Thames was dimly lit, now even darker as the heaviness of the clouds cast a shadow over the city. She stroked a tassel as she rested her head against the velvet curtain, her wig of fiery red hair now dried and loosely fixed on one side of her neck.

Being alone, she allowed her attention to drift as she admired the flowerbeds below, watching them drink in the water that fell from the sky. She was overcome with a sense of peace as her eyes glanced across the river. There was a particularly soothing quality about the way it moved that she couldn't avoid admiring. It was possible she'd never experienced anything more tranquil than the gentle surface of the flowing river.

"There is freedom in the water," she thought, as she considered its movements. Nobody told the river where it had to be, or what it had to do. It moved with the flow, and perhaps that was something a person could envy. Her people obeyed her—countless bodies bowing down at her every command through fear and worship—so why was it that she felt so restricted?

Perhaps she needed to consider the possibility that

2

she'd never really known life. She could have anything—*everything* â€" she wanted, ordered for her without notice, so why did she feel trapped within her own sovereignty?

Her mind weary, she returned her focus to the outdoors as she watched her city absorb the refreshing downpour. She knew there was still some life in her, and while she was still standing nobody could take the beauty of nature from her. She was sure nothing could have disturbed her in that moment.

"Your Majesty?"

The voice had sounded from the end of the corridor. She quickly straightened herself, smoothing down the crease in her skirt. She tucked the loose strand of hair that hung around her face behind her ear and took a step away from the window.

"Lord Burghley?" she addressed the person who had interrupted her. He was a tall man with a nest of greying hair upon his head. "You will be aware that it is quite late. Is there some sort of problem?"

He scurried up the corridor until he was standing nearer to her. Elizabeth again straightened her posture, ensuring her dominance was asserted over him.

"Your Majesty," he spoke as he bowed. He hesitated slightly, having been unprepared to find her standing in the corridor and not in her bedchambers. It had allowed him no time for composure. He neatened his burgundy coat, allowing him a mere second to regain his confidence. "I'm very sorry to disturb you at such an hour, but I am afraid that I must announce that there has been word from Ireland that there are plans for another revolt."

Something told Elizabeth that she should have been shocked by this news, but she would be lying if she said it was not something she had expected.

"And this has been confirmed?"

"Yes, Your Majesty. The leader of this apparent revolt is said to be one Tibbott Bourke. I could not say how many men stand behind him, but I do not think we can

3

afford to take risks. Of course, it is up to you what action is to be taken on this matter, Your Majesty," he added, fearing that he'd overstepped the mark in issuing his own opinion when it was not requested. He continued: "They say there is strength in his parentage. It is possible that he may have an expanding fleet."

"I expect you are right, Lord Burghley. To ensure the safety of my empire, something must be done about this. I will see to it that this Irish brute you speak of is captured and brought to London. I trust you will be able to inform Lord Bingham and instruct him to take the required actions?"

"Right away, Your Majesty." He bowed and started down the corridor.

"And, Lord Burghley,"Elizabeth said, returning her attention to the window, "make sure the boy is brought back alive."

2

Grace clutched onto her handbag as she hurried down Regent Street. It was times like this that she was thankful she didn't really care for wearing heeled shoes, otherwise she would have been severely running the risk of falling flat on her face. It would simply be one more humiliation in her life that she was thankful she could avoid.

She glanced at her watch: five minutes to nine. She knew she should have left earlier to catch the underground. It would be so much easier, she'd always thought, if the Northern line took her directly to Oxford Street. No matter how frequently she'd made the journey though, she always seemed to forget about having to change trains.

A few minutes later, panting as she tried to catch her breath, she reached the main door to the office, a small entrance hidden between two fashion stores. She managed to smile at the receptionist before hurling herself up the stairs.

"Why can't I just take the lift like a normal person?" she grumbled to herself as she puffed her way up another flight. Every day she vowed to get over her fear of lifts—

not only would it be quicker, but it would make getting to work much less of a workout—but she never actually bothered to take any action. Perhaps one day she'd eventually do something about it.

"Probably not though," she confirmed to herself as she finally reached the room. ANCHOR NEWS was written on a piece of A4 in marker pen and proudly stuck to the door with sticky tape to inform visitors of its location. Grace opened the door and slumped inside.

Not surprisingly, she wasn't the first one there.

James was busy grinning at something on his computer monitor. Grace didn't dare to ask what it was this time; he was always trying to get them to view some bizarre video clip or awkward picture on the Internet.

"Morning, James."

"Morning, Grace. Come and have a look at this!"

"Do I even want to know what it is, James?" She dropped her handbag onto her desk.

"Of course you do!" he smirked. "It's a dog wearing a Batman costume. It's wicked!"

She decided not to look at the picture. James continued to grin to himself, his glasses perched on the top of his gelled hair. He was wearing a purple striped jumper this morning, paired with dark skinny jeans. If Grace had to give him credit for anything, it would be the fact that he always took pride in looking smart. Sometimes a little too much pride, but at least he always looked suitable for work. She hadn't expected this from the new boy. Though she did have to wonder, despite the fact that James had been working with the company for six months now, why he was *still* referred to as the new boy. Not that he showed any signs of minding the nickname.

"You know, James," Andy said as he emerged from the coffee machine behind Grace's desk, stirring a cup of black, "you should probably consider pulling up a document or something before Mr Barrie arrives. You know he'll go spare if he catches you looking at anything *fun* online." He turned to Grace: 'Ah, Miss Byrne! Once again you've managed to beat the boss! You didn't happen to see him on your way up, did you?'

'Thankfully not: he was probably right behind me though.'

'Watching your every move?'

'Oh, don't. You'll give me nightmares!'

The office door flung open. A short, round man with a thick moustache walked in, clutching onto a paper bag with a chocolate doughnut inside it. A woman was trailing behind him, carrying a tray of take-away coffees, with a folder of paperwork wedged underneath her arm.

"Good morning, Mr Barrie," Andy spoke to the arrival. He nodded to Fran, who continued to follow the boss to his private office at the back of the room. Once he was out of sight, Andy turned back to Grace and whispered, "Have you ever seen a scowl deeper on a man's forehead before? Something tells me he's not in the best of moods today."

Which, roughly translated, meant that he should be avoided at all costs. Mr Barrie was the sort of boss that demanded respect but never actually earned it. He didn't really do good moods, and today he seemed even less likely to surprise them with a newfound cheery disposition.

"Just what I need; I suppose it's my own fault for expecting any different," Grace joked before finally unbuttoning her coat and hanging it up on the back of her chair.

"Well, we better set things up for this morning's meeting, or you know what will happen."

"He'll chase us all around the building with a carving knife and hack us all into tiny pieces before eating us one by one?"

Andy sniggered. "You have one peculiar imagination, Grace. Still, a part of me worries that you might just be right. Come on, James; time to drag yourself away from your doggy porn and start doing some actual work."

"It's not dog porn, man! This is top quality schnauzer

entertainment!" He pointed to the video clip he was now watching. He turned off the monitor and moved to help Andy assemble the tables and chairs.

Grace placed a chair at the foot of the table, ready to endure the torture of the world's most irritable boss.

"Right, what have you got for me then?" Mr Barrie grumbled once he had joined them.

"Well, I'm still working on the article about the junior football teams you asked for..."

"Thank you, Andy."

James hiccoughed.

"Fran, there are one or two things I'd like you to work on today, but I'll discuss those with you in my office later on." Neither Andy nor James, nor Grace looked up from the table; they all knew what this meant, and chose to ignore it. Fran simply nodded at the boss. "In the meantime, I'd like you to continue with the piece on winter footwear you've been doing."

James hiccoughed again.

"And James—"

Hiccough.

"—will you stop making that stupid noise?!"

"Sorry, sir," he managed, before forcing another one back down his throat.

"You'll continue investigating any breaking news stories, yes?"

"Of course, Mr Barrie."

"And Grace, just keep doing what you usually do. Right! So if everybody knows what they've been assigned, best get on with it then." Mr Barrie hauled his weight out of the tiny chair. The meeting had been exactly the same as it always was. He'd checked to see that everybody knew what he was supposed to be doing, handed out a few instructions, and then told them to go back to their desks. Nobody really knew why they needed to shift the furniture each morning for the sake of a couple of minutes of unneeded instruction, but they were pretty sure it had something to do with Mr Barrie's need for domination. There was nothing they could do about it except rearrange the tables and chairs then shuffle back to their desks to begin yet another day that promised to be identical to the last.

The computer groaned at Grace, once again rebelling against her request. She'd never known a machine to be so averse to sending emails. If only Mr Barrie would update the systems in the office, then perhaps she'd be able to perform her work more efficiently. Finally, the computer informed her that the email had been sent.

She glanced around the office. Everybody seemed hard at work as they typed away, not appearing to be affected by the heavy air that engulfed the room and smothered Grace's good cheer. The clock that hung above the water cooler crawled its way toward the final hour of the work day, and Grace could think of nothing as satisfying as the thought that it was almost time to go home.

The rest of the Anchor team seemed to be of a similar opinion as they rushed to finish their tasks for the day so they could do whatever it was they particularly enjoyed doing outside of work. Grace didn't have any particular plans for the evening, the calendar sitting on her desk informing her that November was as depressingly empty as October had been for her, but anything was better than being stuck inside prison walls. The room was dense with monotony.

She was twiddling her thumbs when Andy walked past, carrying an empty mug in the direction of the kettle in the corner of the room. "Powering through this last article, then I'm off!" he said as he stopped next to her. Andy had already been working for the web site when Grace had joined the team three years ago. In charge of Anchor's sports section, he spent most of his time on location, interviewing young champions or covering the unveiling of new sports centres and academies across London. He enjoyed his job, he would never deny that, but Andy had always hoped he would have moved on from the company to higher positions elsewhere by this stage in his life. He had been in the same role for the same web site for over a decade, having landed his first proper job there once he had graduated from university. By some miracle the bleak office hadn't dampened his ambitions though; he still dreamed of breaking free and climbing higher up the career ladder someday. There were only a certain number of school sports days he could cover before beginning to rethink his entire existence, and that was enough to keep his dream ignited.

"Anything exciting been happening today?" Grace wasn't really into sports, but she always enjoyed talking to Andy regardless of what they were discussing.

"Not particularly. I spent the morning watching a junior cricket match. There were actually some really talented youngsters playing today. I bet they could go far if they chose to. I can only imagine how good they'll be when they hit secondary school. I'm just about finished writing the article." He looked at the mug he was carrying. "One last top-up to help me power through... The sooner we finish the better, eh?"

They exchanged smiles before Andy continued to the kettle. Once he was out of sight Grace allowed her eyes to glance over the rest of the room before they landed on James. As the newest Anchor employee, sitting in front of Andy's desk, he had joined the team six months ago as a Journalism graduate. Barely into his twenties, he still reeked of optimism. Grace was sure working at Anchor would soon suck that zest for life out of him. It was only a matter of time.

Still, she couldn't envy him too much. James was rarely given the chance to parade himself around in public; he was required to spend most of his time stuck in the office. He was responsible for covering all the latest news stories, and always without leaving his desk. He seemed to enjoy working there though. It was all new and exciting to him, his first proper job in the real world, and it did mean he was able to spend a lot of time talking on the phone. He certainly wasn't shy of making a sly personal phone call or two at work either. He had become expert at changing his boyish giggles into a stern offer manner whenever the boss walked into the office. Although he'd frequently come close to it, he'd yet to be caught in the act.

With nothing else to do for the rest of the afternoon, Grace turned away from James and stretched her attention to the far end of the office. Seated at the desk furthest away from Grace was Fran Taylor. Fran was occupying herself by twisting a bottle of clear nail varnish around in one hand, and twirling a strand of her hair with a finger on the other. She had tousled her red hair—dyed, of course—onto the top of her head, leaving a few strands hanging loose by her face to shape her cheekbones. She always wore her hair up, Grace noticed. Why wouldn't she when it made it easier to leave her chest exposed for the world to see? Fran was quite short in height, but curved and relatively busty. Grace couldn't avoid noting that Fran's blouse was stretched across her chest, the maroon silk fabric pulling at the top button, threatening to pop off at any moment. Grace was sure she'd end up taking a button to the eye one of these days, especially with the way Fran spent more time than necessary leaning over desks and forcing her breasts forward. She always liked to keep her legs on display too, dressing them in a pair of flimsy tights and pairing them with nude shoes in an attempt to lengthen their appearance. On more occasions than she could count, Grace had caught Mr Barrie staring at Fran's shapely legs as they stretched out from under her tiny skirts.

More like belts, Grace caught herself thinking as she spotted the size of Fran's skirt of choice that day. She didn't know why she even bothered wearing them; they barely covered anything.

It hadn't come as any surprise to Grace when she learned that Fran was in charge of writing about the latest fashion and beauty news. Although she avoided conversations with Fran at all costs, Grace had to admit that she admired Fran's ability to write extensively about celebrity faux pas. Grace simply didn't care about the latest must-have handbag, or which shade of denim goes best with green eyes. She never understood the vast desperation for fashion, and she didn't really wish to either.

Just as she was stifling a yawn, Grace noticed out of the corner of her eye that an email had popped up on the screen. She dragged her body around to face the machine, trying to feign an interest. It was probably just another offer for Fran to test out some new cosmetics line. It was never anything for Grace.

She was certain she wasn't in the position she had originally applied for at Anchor, but however it had happened, she now found herself responding to all of the emails that were received. She found no satisfaction in the mind-numbing repetition of clicking and forwarding. Her thoughts even started to echo the low drone of the machines that filled the air around her, anything to occupy the vacant space that increasingly grew inside her head with each tediously dull moment. And, as the online news site wasn't exactly popular, very few people ever had a need to email with general enquires for Grace to answer. On the rare occasion that they did, it was usually with a question that had already been answered on the site's designated section for Frequently Asked Questions. Copying and pasting answers wasn't exactly what Grace had dreamed of doing all her life.

Maybe, if she was completely honest, she envied the rest of the team. A tiny part of her was even jealous of Fran, but she would never admit that to her face. The rest were always hard at work on their projects within their own specialties, and here she was about to read yet another email that was going to offer absolutely no fulfillment to her.

"So much excitement I can barely contain myself," she sighed as she faced the monitor.

She recognised the name instantly. To her surprise the email *was* for her. However, when she read the subject line, she almost wished it wasn't. She opened the email:

Gracey, darling!

How are you? I'm hosting a lingerie party tomorrow at my place for all my girlfriends. You absolutely must come! You still have my address don't you? I'll see you tomorrow around 7. Oh, and do bring Harriet—there'll be plenty of nibbles for everybody!

Love Caroline xxx

She decided that no email would definitely have been better than this. She'd completely forgotten that Caroline even knew her work email. It had been so long since she'd heard from her. She was obviously struggling to make up numbers for the party otherwise there was no way Grace would have been invited.

Caroline Abbott had been on Grace's course at university, and they'd ended up being paired together for various projects. It wasn't that Grace didn't like Caroline. She just found her hard to handle. It didn't help that Caroline was now working for a much more acclaimed company than Grace was—at least Caroline's work made it to print every week. Perhaps it had something to do with the fact that she was lively and full of character, and not actually a lot to do with her writing ability. Regardless of whether or not Grace was bitter, sometimes Caroline was just too full-on for Grace's liking.

If she didn't go to the party though, she'd never hear the end of it. Sometimes it was easier to give in to Caroline than to try and avoid her.

"Anything for a peaceful life," she muttered as she typed out a quick reply to Caroline. "At least it'll get me out of the house for a few hours, I suppose—"even if it *is* to a lingerie party." It wasn't usually her scene, but it had to be better than spending another night in front of the TV nursing an oversized cup of hot chocolate. Her Saturdays were starting to become entirely too routine.

She had just responded to the email when Mr Barrie's office door swung open. He stormed out with a piece of paper in his hand and headed toward Andy's desk.

Once he had finished with Andy—Grace had tried to eavesdrop but his tone was too low—he turned his attention to her as she tried to avoid his stare.

"Working hard, are we, Grace?"

"Yes, sir."

"Well, you've still got another ten minutes to get everything finished for today. You can leave when the clock hits five. And not a minute sooner," he ordered before making his way to a bag of mini cupcakes next to the kettle that Andy had brought in from the supermarket at lunch time. He grabbed one with lemon icing and stuffed a bite into his mouth. Crumbs flaked down his shirt. He patted at it with a meaty hand, trying not to smear icing over the taut fabric. He shuffled back to his office, smiling at the cupcake.

Grace spent the final ten minutes staring at the clock. She had to resist the temptation to cheer when the second hand crawled up to the final ten seconds before the top of the hour, fighting the urge to commence a full countdown. She shut down her computer and stood, sliding her arms into her coat at the same time. "See you on Monday, Andy."

"See you," he replied as he shut off his machine. No matter how busy they had been in the minutes leading up to the end of the day, nobody ever chose to stay longer than they had to.

"Bye, James."

Grace picked up her bag and headed out the door. She made her way down the stairs, a journey much less exhausting and much more exciting than the ascent, and turned to exit the building.

Fran stood in the doorway, holding a cigarette loosely between two fingers. Grace tried to ignore her as she stopped to button her coat.

"You know, if you made more of an effort, then he might let you do more," Fran smirked as she blew smoke in front of her. The chill of the wind didn't seem to bother her as she stood there in her skimpy outfit, her legs and chest exposed.

"Sorry?" Grace responded, confused. She hadn't expected Fran to say anything to her. They rarely spoke to each other, engaging in conversation only when it was necessary.

"Look at you, Grace." Fran gestured toward Grace's outfit with her cigarette. Grace was aware that her grey trousers were a little plain, and her woolly coat was perhaps a little oversized, but it had been on sale when she bought it. Besides, she had never considered her wardrobe to be a problem.

"Don't think I haven't noticed you in there," Fran continued. "I've overheard your conversations with Andy. I know you don't feel challenged enough. Am I right?"

"Well, maybe..." Grace wasn't sure where Fran was going with this. She had never cared about her feelings before. Why was she taking an interest now?

"I know Arthur, Grace..." Grace shuddered at the sound of Mr Barrie's first name. It made him human, which of course was impossible. "...and I also know he's not going to consider your talents as a writer if you don't start making more of an effort with your appearance. I mean, take me, for example." Fran flicked the ash from her cigarette onto the floor. "He's given me more creative freedom than I could ever have asked for. Just last week I attended a press event for a boutique in Kensington. They loved me so much that they gave me this expensive dress with the most gorgeous little straps as a gift to say thank you for writing about them. Seriously, ditch this little girl look and try something a bit more womanly. It's the only way you're ever going to get anywhere in life." Fran stubbed out the end of her cigarette against the wall and threw the butt onto the floor. 'See you next week,' she grinned as she turned back into the building.

Grace stood still for a moment as she tried to take in what Fran had just said to her. The wind picked up around her, causing her to shudder. She drew the belt of her coat tighter around her and turned to walk up Regent Street toward the underground station. The sooner she shook away the sound of Fran's voice the better. Grace knew she was only trying to manipulate her. She couldn't let anything that Fran had said affect her. She tried to block out her words as she powered up the hill, getting as far away from the Anchor office as possible.

3

Grace stuffed her Oyster card back into her purse and headed out of the station. The road was surprisingly quiet for that time of the evening, as she found out when she managed to cross to the other side without having to wait at the traffic lights. Instead of being lit by the usual stream of headlights, however, the silver moon glistening in the blue-black of the night sky provided a soft, almost-magical glow across Hampstead.

It was only when Grace turned left down Rosslyn Hill that she spotted the pattern of stars above her. The nights had started to turn darker much earlier now that winter was fast approaching. The air was noticeably colder, and Grace was sure that it was going to start raining at any moment. She prayed she was wrong though, as her umbrella was hidden somewhere at the bottom of her bag. Plus, she'd taken a detour this evening, adding time to her journey home.

After a tiresome day she decided she was in need of some comfort. Had she thought about it before the Tube had pulled away from the previous station—her typical luck, she acknowledged—she would have gotten off at

Belsize Park to save some leg work. But apparently that wasn't how this day was meant to go. She'd originally planned to continue reading the paperback she'd begun the night before, but the drone that engulfed the office had given her an awful headache; the last thing she felt like doing was concentrating on the tiny print of *Great Expectations*, however hooked to the story she was.

Instead, she emerged onto Haverstock Hill and continued down the road until she arrived at her destination.

"Portion of chips, please," she requested. "Large."

She paid for the chips, left the chip shop, and clutched onto the steaming bag for warmth as she braved the cold. It would take her only ten minutes to walk home, and she hoped that her comfort food wouldn't be stone cold by the time she arrived.

As she made her way up the hill Grace noticed how empty the streets seemed. It was almost eerie. *The calm before the storm*, she thought to herself. The wind blew lightly, barely enough to ruffle the ends of her scarf. A woman was walking briskly down the other side of the road, clutching onto an oversized bottle-green patent leather handbag, her heels echoing on the pavement as she walked. A young child ahead was bundled inside a padded winter coat with her face hardly visible, hidden beneath the hood's fur trim. The child's mother was frantically stuffing mittens onto her hands as they both moved along in unison. There was nobody else in sight. Although she had expected it to be busier on a Friday evening, she couldn't deny that she was enjoying the peace.

Her mind had started to relax so much, in fact, that she hadn't noticed that the inevitable had happened: it was raining. It wasn't until she watched the young girl's mother wrestling with an umbrella as she tried not to drop her shopping bags that Grace actually took note of the first rain drop to fall onto her shoulder. It was followed almost immediately by another. Not wishing to take any chances at the risk of soaking her food parcel, she quickened up her pace as the rain began to fall harder. By the time she came to her turning near the top of Haverstock Hill, the water had started lashing down on top of her. Hugging the chips tightly to her chest, she could do nothing but run the rest of the way home.

The door locked itself behind her as she threw her keys back into her bag. She shook her head, trying to cast away the water that was now dripping down her face. "I'm so glad I keep my hair up," Grace mumbled to herself as she dabbed at the back of her bun with the sleeve of her coat before hanging it up on the banister at the bottom of the stairs. By the time she'd arrived just moments after the heavens had opened, the front of her house had become decorated with streaks from the downpour.

"Is that you, Grace?" The muffled voice came from the living room.

"It's me, don't worry Harriet."

She turned into the living room to find Harriet sprawled across the sofa in her pyjamas, a glass of red wine in one hand and a bag of popcorn in the other. A tabby cat was stretched across Harriet's legs, sound asleep.

"Been home long?"

"About half an hour." She noticed the drowned rat appearance Grace was sporting. "Raining?"

"Only buckets." Grace sat on the smaller sofa as Harriet shoved another handful of popcorn into her mouth.

"Want one?" The cat miaowed when Harriet turned her body to face Grace. 'Quiet, Bella,' she said as she petted the cat between the ears to stroke it back to sleep.

"No thanks," Grace replied, rejecting the sweetened offerings that had been thrust in her direction. She pulled the chip box out of the paper bag and let the warmth smother her face. She was relieved to see it hadn't been affected by the rain as she inhaled deeply to allow the hot aromas of salt and vinegar to fill her nostrils. There was something so comforting about chip shop chips that she could never quite put her finger on. She could think of nothing like it. As she bit into a steaming chip, she instantly forgot about the lousy weather and her boring plans for yet another mundane evening.

"What are you watching?" she finally asked as she nodded towards the TV screen. A pile of Harriet's DVDs lay next to the TV.

"A film." She threw a piece of popcorn at Grace and stuck out her tongue.

"I know that much! What's it about?" Harriet was in one of these moods. Grace guessed she'd been stood up again; snacking seemed to be Harriet's method for cheering herself up.

Maybe one day she'll realise he's not right for her, Grace thought to herself.

"I'm not going to tell you what it's about. You'll just have to sit here with me and watch it to find out for yourself."

Grace didn't want to leave Harriet on her own when she was feeling like this, but her headache was rapidly growing worse and she knew that staring at a TV screen wasn't going to do her any good. "I'd love to Harriet, but I think I'm just going to eat these and have an early night."

"I know how you feel."

She chewed away on the rest of the chips, comfortably tucked into the corner of the sofa. Once she was finished, she scrunched the paper bag into a ball and sighed.

"Well, I suppose I should head upstairs..." She forced herself out of the seat as she watched a pale-faced woman dance across the screen with a tray of pies. The film was actually quite good, but she knew she had to be sensible and occupy herself upstairs where the darkness would help soothe her aching head.

"I need more wine," Harriet said as she stood up, sending Bella shooting onto the floor. The cat licked her paw and skulked out of the room. "Here, give me that," Harriet said as she gestured towards the empty chip box in Grace's hand.

"Thanks," Grace replied, handing the rubbish to her. Harriet firmly held onto her empty wine glass in her free hand as she took everything to the kitchen.

Grace turned and stared at the pile of books sitting at the foot of the sofa. She'd left them there the previous evening when she'd attempted to organise them, having planned to donate some to the charity shop. She'd given up half way through sorting though.

'I think I'll keep them all for now,' she said as she shuffled as much of the pile together as she could carry.

She tried to balance them in her arms as she made her way up the stairs, taking each step slowly to avoid sending the paperbacks flying. Once she reached her room, she released them onto her bed, allowing them to spread out.

"I didn't really think this through, did I?"

The lack of storage space was precisely the reason why she'd instructed herself to give some of the books to a charity in the first place. Her reluctance to part with even one now meant she was back to square one. She scratched at her head, pondering. The drying rain water had left her hair feeling like straw. She'd deal with the books later. First she needed to shower.

She grabbed a towel from the linen cupboard and headed into the bathroom, locking the door behind her. Padding her bare feet across the navy tiles she stopped in front of the cabinet and took out her toothbrush. The chips had left a foul aftertaste in her mouth, the sort that started out satisfying but later served as a reminder of why takeaways weren't the healthiest of options.

She scrubbed, spat, and rinsed before returning the toothbrush to the cupboard. She stared at her own reflection in the mirror, studying the wisps of hair that had escaped from her bun. Dark circles had started to emerge under her eyes.

Maybe Fran's right.

She didn't know where the thought had come from. Until now she'd successfully managed to ignore the conversation they'd had outside the office earlier that evening. Why she'd thought of it now, she couldn't tell.

Why don't you just give it a go?

The voice was coaxing her from the back of her mind. Suddenly it didn't seem like such a bad idea. She reached into the bathroom cabinet and produced a green drawstring bag that had been there since she'd moved in six years ago.

She emptied the contents of the make-up bag onto the side of the sink. Only a few items tumbled out: a pot of foundation that had dried up years ago; a mascara that had clumped up at the bottom of the tube; a few crumbling pots of eye shadow; a stick of cream blusher she'd never used, and half a lipstick in a black case that was caked in fingerprints. A rush of nostalgia came over her as she thought back to the last time she'd seen the collection. It must have been 2007, and she'd managed to land herself a date with a colleague from the coffee shop she used to work at part-time. What was his name? Nathan? Nigel? Something like that... She struggled to remember it now. He was cute though, and she had wanted to impress him, so she decided that she would experiment with cosmetics. Whether or not it had anything to do with make-up, they never did go on a second date.

She picked up one of the eye shadows and opened the lid, releasing a small cloud of pink dust into the air.

Perhaps if I just...

She swiped a finger across the product and smeared it over her eye lid, coating it in pastel pink. She repeated the step on her other eye and blinked a few times to shake off the excess dust.

Without thinking about what she was doing, she reached for the lipstick, taking her time to twist the bottom to reveal the fuchsia colour. She drew her hand to her mouth and began to drag it across her bottom lip, continuing all the way round in one movement until she'd coloured in her top lip too. She returned the lipstick to the container while rubbing her lips together.

Her eyes were wide as she picked up the stick of blusher. The creamy champagne colour was speckled with shimmer, supposedly to dazzle onlookers whenever it caught the light. Grace placed it flat on her face and swirled repeatedly until both of her cheeks displayed circles of shiny pink.

She stared into the mirror to study her new look. The shades clashed as the thickly-coated products fought against one another to stand out. Against her naturally pale skin, anyone could have mistaken her image as a preparation for a clown college.

A single tear trickled down Grace's face as she rushed to bundle the products back into the bag before reaching for the facecloth. She ran it under the tap and began scrubbing profusely at her cheeks. Now tears were streaming down her face as she rubbed harder, the colours smearing across her skin and mixing together, harsh and unsightly.

She turned on the shower and stripped out of her clothes. She had no idea what had come over her. She never should have listened to Fran. She knew it was foolish of her. So why did she feel so pathetic?

After releasing her hair from its bun so that her auburn waves cascaded down her back, she stood under the running water. The radio was turned on to drown out the sound of her emotions. She was still for a moment as she let the warm water cover her. She soaked the body puff in shower gel and lathered it before scrubbing her entire body and hopefully cleansing herself of all negative thoughts. In fact, she worked furiously to erase what had happened. She didn't stop until her tears had been washed away, and the Grace that she knew had been fully restored.

As she made her way into her bedroom, she pulled the cord tighter around her dressing gown. She had towel-dried her hair after her shower, so it was now once again wrapped in a bun at the back of her head. It had been exactly what she had needed; she felt so much more refreshed now, and was a lot less anxious than she had been less than an hour ago.

"Now where did I put it?" Feeling more relaxed she was finally in the mood to sit under the duvet with a book. She rummaged at the collapsed pile on the bed, but there was no sign of a Dickens novel.

"Ah, the wardrobe..." She crossed to the other side of the room and flung back the wardrobe door and a pile of paperbacks tumbled out and fell against her slippers, jabbing at her bare heel. She rubbed it to ease the pain. "This is never going to work, is it?" She scooped up the pile and hugged it to her chest.

Mentally scanning the entire house, she searched for somewhere suitable to store them. It wouldn't be fair of her to simply dump them in the living room where Harriet spent a lot of time too, and she never did get around to buying the book case for the hallway that she'd promised herself several years back. She scuttled onto the landing with the books and stood at the top of the stairs. "Maybe if I just move some of the towels in the linen cupboard, I could squeeze—"

She had to scramble to stop the books from falling from her arms. Her attention had been caught by surprise as her eyes bolted toward the wall at the top of the stairs.

Why hadn't she seen it before? Surely it was something she would have noticed before now? She left the books in a pile on the floor and crossed over the landing, not once allowing herself to take her eyes off the wall.

In the six years she'd lived in Hampstead the house had never been redecorated. She often thought it needed refreshing, but nothing was ever done about it, so the same blue and cream pinstriped wallpaper remained in the downstairs hallway and stretched up to the upstairs landing. It was nothing fancy, but it did the job.

Except now there was a door handle sticking out of the wall. Grace studied the circular knob that protruded through the wallpaper. It wasn't huge, of course, but who wouldn't notice a doorknob sticking out of their wall?

It was only when she finally averted her eyes and cast them around the surrounding area that she noticed the rest. A rectangular shape took form in the wallpaper, as if somebody had used a knife to mark out the outline of a door. The lines were sharp and parallel; almost completely hidden.

Maybe there *was* a cupboard here all along, Grace thought. But why would the landlord paper over it? "Harriet!" she shouted down the stairs, "do you know if there are other cupboards upstairs apart from the one we keep the towels in?" It seemed like a mad question to ask.

"Just the one I'm afraid! Why?" The voice drifted up from the living room.

"Nothing important... I was just looking for somewhere to store my books," she managed to answer.

That settled it: Harriet hadn't seen the door either.

She reached out her hand and placed it on the doorknob. Almost as quickly, she drew her hand back. Her fingers had collided with something.

Peering beneath the doorknob introduced her to a surge of emotions. She sighed, relieved to find that it was only a key she'd touched.

But why would there be a key for a cupboard like this?

The linen cupboard didn't lock, and none of the other doors in the house apart from the front and back doors came with keys. Curious, she pulled it out and placed it in her palm.

It was black and rusted, and stretched the entire length of her hand. It was thin, narrow, and had a little hoop on the end of it so that it could be hung somewhere, or perhaps attached to a piece of ribbon. The metal felt cold against her skin.

She drew it back to the lock and manoeuvred it around, struggling to get it back into the keyhole. It felt quite uneven, probably because of the cobwebs that had formed an additional layer inside the lock which had to be penetrated before the door could be opened. Grace had no idea what to expect on the other side.

Finally, the key clicked into place. Grace slowly turned it counter-clockwise until it clicked a second time, a signal that the door was now unlocked. She left the key in the keyhole and placed a hand on the doorknob. It had turned cold, much colder than she had expected. She turned the knob and pulled gently.

There was a creak as the door moved.

Grace stood back and pulled the door further. It was now completely open. The wallpaper on the front of the door, she noticed, remained intact; it didn't rip or tear at all as the rectangle came away from the wall. She braced herself as she peered inside.

The cupboard was completely dark.

That's odd, she thought, noticing that none of the light from the hallway seemed to penetrate the recess. There was no way of telling how deep it was, or whether or not there were shelves for her books.

At the bottom left corner of the cupboard, however, Grace noticed a small thread of light fighting its way through the darkness; it seemed to be coming from the bathroom.

There must be a hole in the back of the cupboard, she decided, but she was certain that she hadn't left the bathroom light on.

There was a gentle shuffling sound coming from behind her. She turned to see that it was only Bella coming up the stairs. She paused at the top step to lick her paws.

"Up to your usual tricks again, Bella?"

The mischievous cat didn't bother to acknowledge the accusation. She stood on all fours and continued on toward Harriet's bedroom.

Bella was the sort of animal that ignored the old saying, *curiosity killed the cat*. She was a springy animal, always exploring. They'd once caught her stuck in a large flowerpot when she was a kitten, obviously trapped after one of her adventures had gone wrong. Any sign of new territory and she had to stick her paws in it. It was completely out of her nature to ignore the before unseen cupboard in front of her. In fact, it was as if she hadn't seen the cupboard at all.

Grace convincing herself it was nothing to be concerned about, and turned her attention to the dark shape in front of her. Since she couldn't see anything in the darkness, she decided she was just going to have to feel for the depth of the cupboard with her hands. She took a step closer and reached her arm out.

It must be deeper than I expected, she told herself. I can't seem to feel the back wall yet. She moved one foot inside the space as she edged closer.

Finally, she pressed her hand against something firm: the back wall. She brought her other hand forward so she could push both palms against the surface. It felt like wood, not the brickwork she had imagined. Just as soon as she had considered this to be quite peculiar, the golden thread of light in the left corner began to worm its way along the edge where the wall met the floor, growing until it reached the opposite side. Grace glanced down, her eyes widening.

A strange wind began to pick up inside the cupboard, swirling a cold breeze around her. It seemed to be coming from the direction of the back wall, but she'd just confirmed that the wall was solid. How could this be possible?

She was about to run out of the cupboard, but the thought had occurred to her too late. The door slammed shut behind her, camouflaging itself once again as it blended into the wallpaper. There was no time to panic as the wooden panels that had once posed as the back wall shifted from beneath Grace's hands, plunging her deeper into the darkness.

4

As she emerged on the other side, the light nearly blinded her. It only lasted a second. She had stumbled as she'd fallen through the cupboard, losing her balance as the back wall had disappeared right under her grasp. She stood now, having just managed to regain her equilibrium. She wondered for a moment if she had perhaps taken a bump to the head. Maybe this was all a dream, or some crazy concussion-induced hallucination. She told herself that it wasn't likely, but neither was the other option she had to consider: that she'd just fallen through a mysterious cupboard in her own home that she'd never before seen. She quite clearly remembered holding the key, and the door had definitely been cut out of the wallpaper at the top of the stairs. She had no idea where she was. Something told her she was no longer in Hampstead though, and she desperately needed to find out what was going on.

The only source of light seemed to be coming from a candle situated in the corner of the room. In order to gain a better view of her new surroundings, she would need to fetch the candle and guide the light directly in front of her.

But that would require her to cross over to it, and she had no idea whether or not that was going to put her in danger. She remained rooted to the spot where she stood for a few minutes as she frantically tried to come up with an alternative solution, but she soon had to face the truth. There *was* no alternative. Her only option was to fetch the candlestick. Not without hesitation, she allowed her right foot to slide forward an inch. When she was relieved to find that it didn't collide with anything, she moved her left foot so that they were together again. The floor was rough, uneven, and painful on her bare skin. She guessed it was wooden, and began to worry that splinters would cut into her feet. But she had to get to the candle. With nothing in her path, she continued to move her feet one at a time, ensuring that her steps were soft and silent. Several moments later, she was standing directly in front of the candle.

She tried not to move too swiftly as she reached for the candlestick. There already seemed to be a draft in the room, and any sudden movements could cost her the only source of light. She lifted it and turned to face the centre of the room.

Her eyes widened as she took in her surroundings, which were now softly illuminated by the candle's glow. It appeared to Grace that she was standing in some sort of narrow cabin. As she had surmised, the floors were made from wood, with the panelling of the walls made from the same material. The rough splinters surrounding her could be noticed even in the dim candlelight.

A bed was situated in the far corner of the room, opposite to where she now stood. It was a peculiar size, much smaller than the single bed she'd had as a child, and much lower to the ground too. She steadied her breathing and moved closer to it, still clutching onto the candlestick. As she leaned over and placed her hand flat against the bed sheet, she confirmed to herself that it was real.

It was becoming increasingly more challenging to

convince herself that she was simply experiencing some peculiar dream—or maybe a nightmare, she couldn't quite tell which. She lifted her hand off the bed. The surface beneath the sheet was solid, and certainly uncomfortable. Grace wondered how anybody could sleep there.

She turned to take in the rest of the room. There was not a lot to see. Next to the table bearing the candle was a small wooden chest. The metal rings on the top shone as the light of the candle reflected off them. Enticed, she walked over to it and knelt down in front of it. She tried to open the chest with one hand but the lid was too heavy. Setting the candle on the floor beside her so that both of her hands were free, she pressed her palms onto the wood and gripped the metal rings. She struggled with its weight until the lid began to move. It creaked as she lifted until it was fully open.

At once she dropped the lid, letting it crash down.

What she'd seen had frightened her. The chest was almost empty, but the candlelight had managed to seek out the only object inside. A sword stretched the length of the chest, a warning for any intruder.

Where on earth am I?

She stumbled onto her feet and straightened herself up, lifting the candle with her. As the fear grew inside her, she knew she had to get out of this place.

She was about to head for the door behind her when she paused. It had taken her a moment to realise that she was heading for a different door. This was not the door through which she'd entered. She turned to find the other door against the wall near the bed: the entrance that had brought her here.

She left the candle in the centre of the floor so that it would cast just enough light throughout the entire room, setting it down so that it wouldn't topple over. She approached the door and placed her hand on the doorknob.

She turned it. Nothing happened.

She tried to push the door, but it wouldn't budge. She fought and shook with all her might but still it would not cooperate. She was trapped.

Thinking quickly, she decided that there was only one thing to do: Unless she wanted to spend the rest of her life stuck inside this strange room, she was going to have to try the other door.

"It's now or never," she whispered to herself as she lifted her hand toward the new doorknob. She turned it, carefully rotating it counter-clockwise.

The door clicked as it released, a strand of light appearing through the crack in the opening. A draught hissed through the gap as well. Grace stepped back, pulling the door open further. She decided not to open it all the way since she had no idea what lay on the other side, and there was every possibility that she'd need to quickly shut it again. But it was a risk she was going to have to take. Whatever happened, she had to finding answers.

Angling her body, she slipped through the gap and left the room behind.

She was almost blinded by the sunlight as she emerged on the other side of the threshold. She blinked to shield her eyes until they had adjusted to the brightness. A sigh of relief washed over her when she realised that she was outside. If nothing else, being out in the open didn't make her feel as suffocated.

When she was finally able to fully open her eyes again, she couldn't quite believe what she was seeing. What lay before her had taken her by surprise, perhaps even captivated her. It appeared that she was now standing on a ship, its entire length stretching out from where she stood.

Turning to check what was behind her she noticed the cabin from which she'd just emerged. There was a large wheel positioned to her right as it stood motionless. Was this supposed to make sense to her? Was she supposed to understand why she was here? If she climbed down onto the main deck, maybe something would become clearer.

She reached the last rung of the ladder and landed with a thud. She turned and stared the length of the ship. Thick masts stood at the centre, each one situated in front of the other. In the middle, the tallest of the three stretched toward the sky. As she approached it, Grace reached out to touch it, only to find that it was a lot smoother than she had imagined it to be. She allowed her eyes to follow its height as she traced it toward the clouds. She had to place a hand over the top of her eyes to shield them from the brightness of the sun, its warmth beating down directly onto the ship. The clouds, white and fluffy, rested peacefully in the blue blanket that gazed back at her.

Grace took a step sideways, her attention remaining on the top of the mast, when she bumped into something at the foot of the tall pole. She turned to find a stump on the floor, around which a length of thick rope was coiled. She followed it to discover that it stretched right up the mast to the very top. It was attached to something but Grace couldn't quite make out what it was at first.

Of course! It's the sail!

Hanging loose and wrapped around the masts, she wondered how they'd look when unfurled and ready to take the wind.

Continuing down the deck, the ship appeared to be deserted. Where was the crew and the captain?

"I'm not imagining this," Grace told herself.

She moved to the other side of the ship and leaned upon a shallow wooden ledge. She gripped onto it to balance herself and leaned over, looking out at the ocean. It seemed never ending. In the distance she was sure she could see something—land of some sort, an island perhaps. As she watched the sun reflect its daylight against the surface of the water she realised that she no longer felt as scared as she had at first. She still had lot of questions needing answers, but she had become so mesmerised by the gentle waves as she listened to them lapping against the hull beneath her that, if even for a moment, everything seemed peaceful.

A gull circled and squawked loudly overhead, snapping her attention back to her surroundings. She shot her head up toward the sky as she watched it fly directly above her and out to sea. She turned so that she could look in the direction from which it had come only to determine that the ship was not out at sea but actually anchored in a harbour.

Without giving it a second thought, she stepped onto the gangway. Her hands hovered to the sides automatically to maintain her balance as she walked down the plank, leaving the ship behind her. She tried not to remind herself that she was moving further and further away from the door that had brought her to this place. She didn't really know what to think any more, and she certainly wasn't sure what was she was doing here, but it was time for her to explore.

Once she reached the pier, she stood with the ship standing enormous behind her.

Wherever she was, it was very beautiful. The grass that stretched out in front of her was a rich green and blended into a strand that outlined the water. Grace watched for a moment as the bright waves flowed up the little beach before ebbing to join the sea again.

She decided it was time to continue walking. Not that there was any other option since it didn't seem she'd be able to get back home any time soon. The land grew into hills in front of her. It made sense to her that she should climb one of them.

She started up a path, taking caution with her steps as she walked. She took her time as a comforting wind helped her to travel up the slope of the hill. Once she reached the top she found that the land wasn't as empty as she had first thought. A small cluster of houses were situated in front of her. She wasn't close enough for anybody to notice her standing there, so she assumed that she could study them safely out of sight.

She counted the four houses. They were low to the ground, suggesting that they only had one floor, and were built from large blocks of some kind. Even from where she stood she could tell that the houses were weathered. Since they were situated right by the sea, however, it didn't help her to identify their age. Perhaps they had been worn much more quickly being subjected to the salty air.

Regardless, she was certain she wasn't in the twenty-first century any more. The thatched roofs definitely suggested otherwise. They had probably once been the product of fine craftsmanship, neat and tidy and in order, but now they looked weak and not enough to withstand a heavy downpour.

But where were the inhabitants? Either they were inside their homes, or this land was completely deserted. As she glanced around she spotted something on a nearby mound. Standing near the side of the ship, which remained not too far away behind her, the building was a similar grey to that of the houses, and looked as if it were carefully situated to guard the vessel. Thin and almost square in shape, it was somewhat taller than the houses.

It must have at least three floors, Grace thought to herself as she observed the building from a distance. For reasons she couldn't explain, she felt drawn to it.

"There you are!"

Grace jumped, startled. She had been preparing herself to make her way across the hill so she could observe the building up close when somebody had crept up behind her. She wasn't alone after all.

As the shock of the stranger approaching from behind her subsided, she turned to find a young girl standing nearby. She was a little shorter than Grace, and her hair was brown, shoulder length and curled at the sides of her cheeks. Her delicate features suggested that she couldn't be any older than sixteen.

The girl wore a dress that reached to her ankles, a white cloth decorated with a simple frill at the hem. Over her shoulders she had wrapped a woollen shawl. It was a warm day, but the thin material was enough to keep the wind away from her otherwise-bare arms.

It was only then that Grace noticed her own clothes. She had been so transfixed by the strangeness of her new surroundings that she hadn't realised that she was no longer wearing her pink pyjamas, nor had she physically felt anything strange that might have prompted her to pay attention to her own appearance.

She stood there now wearing an outfit she knew she had most certainly never seen before. A skirt the colour of copper flowed down to her ankles. A white chemise was tucked into the skirt, its long sleeves reaching her wrists; a tan bodice was laced over the chemise, the black string pulling the soft fabric together and leaving just enough room for Grace to breathe without feeling suffocated.

Still bemused by her sudden change of outfit, and equally confused about the fact that she'd only just now noticed it, she turned her attention to the girl, who was still smiling at her.

"Donal wishes to know what time you plan to leave."

Donal? What was she supposed to say to that? She had no idea who this girl was. She definitely didn't know who Donal was. She didn't even know *how* she could leave, never mind what time she planned on doing so.

"Donal?" She risked the question. She considered the girl's thick accent for a moment—it was definitely Irish, but with her mind already racing with a thousand thoughts she struggled to place it more specifically.

"Your brother, of course! I think you've been spending too much time in the sunlight." The girl's smile merged into a chuckle. She must have thought Grace was playing games. But how did she know who Grace was?

"He sent me up here to ask you," the girl continued. "He told me, 'If I know my sister, Miss O'Flynn, then I bet she'll be busy with the ship.' I just said to him, 'please, Donal! You must call me Cathleen!' But you know what your brother's like. He insisted on calling me Miss O'Flynn. I do not care for it much myself, but it is ever so sweet of him. He was right about you, though. He knew I'd find you up here!"

Grace was thankful that this girl seemed to be extremely talkative. It meant she didn't have the chance to explain that she had no idea what was going on.

"So what will I tell him then?"

Grace couldn't keep up with the conversation as she had begun to worry about how she was going to get home. She was even starting to consider the possibility that she might never see London again.

"What time have you decided to leave? He suggested leaving early in the evening, as it would mean you'd be able to rest during the night, but he said it was up to you. You are the captain, after all!"

I'm the what?!

"Although, may I suggest that you find some shoes, Miss Granuaile?" Cathleen giggled as she looked down at Grace's feet.

Miss who?!

Grace was growing increasingly confused by the minute. She looked down at her feet to find that they were still bare, just as the girl had indicated. She wiggled her toes and felt the grass beneath her feet for the first time. It was cold and slightly damp.

"Yes, I'll find some shoes." She considered explaining everything to Cathleen, but she wasn't even sure which century she was in, and explaining that she was almost certain that she'd arrived from the future, however it had happened, wasn't going to get her anywhere either. Her life might even be at risk. She needed to get away from this girl before she found out that Grace was not who she thought she was.

Her mind raced as she searched for a way out, then she remembered the boots. Hadn't there been a pair of boots beside the chest in the room on the ship through which she'd entered? Brown leather boots. If she put those on, then Cathleen would be less likely to get suspicious. At least that was her hope, and that might buy Grace some time to come up with a plan to get back home.

"I must have taken them off when I was on the ship. I'll fetch them now." She began to walk backwards as she spoke.

"I'll see you, Miss Gráinne!" Cathleen laughed as she waved, watching as Grace turned and made for the ship.

She stumbled down the hill, catching herself before she fell. Her heart was racing. She was just about to board the ship when she paused. She hadn't noticed it before, but there was something written on the side of it: *The Pirate Queen*.

Grace stared at the letters for a moment, wondering what the name meant. She'd never really considered the stories behind the names of vessels before, but something told her to pay attention to this one. So many questions whirled in her mind. What was the significance of the *Pirate Queen*? Was it named after anybody? Why had she found herself inside a cabin on this ship, and why was it connected to her home in Hampstead? *Things like this just don't happen!*

She moved across the gangplank and jumped onto the deck. Speeding by the masts and manoeuvring around crates, she didn't stop until she'd reached the ladders leading to the cabin. She bolted through the door and entered the room. The candle was still burning at the centre; Grace was sure it had melted only a small amount despite the length of time she'd been away. It was still glowing as brightly now as it had been when she'd left it.

Her memory had served her well. In the corner of the room, almost hidden beside the chest, stood the pair of boots she had recalled. Grace reached for them, fearing time was running out, and pulled one toward her. She slid her hand inside the narrow neck of the boot to part it so that her foot could be inserted with ease, but as she did this her hand encountered something inside. Grace pulled her hand back and looked inside the boot, but it was too dark to see anything; whatever she'd touched was in the toe. She felt around for the mysterious object. She found it and pulled it out.

She clutched onto a piece of paper. It had been folded and was crumpled slightly where she had pushed it further inside the boot. She unfolded it, making sure she was careful not to tear it.

It looked like a note of some kind. Grace had to move closer to the candle to make out the scrawl; the handwriting was a peculiar script, old fashioned and difficult to read.

The moment she began to see it by candlelight, however, she dropped it onto the floor. It wasn't just a note, but a letter addressed to Miss Grace Byrne.

Her name now staring up at her from where it had fallen to the ground, Grace's fear grew within her as she found herself trapped in a world, and in a time, and in a life that was not her own.

Only then did she notice that the door in the corner of the room, the door through which she had originally entered, was now open slightly. This was her chance— maybe her only chance—she had to leave now.

Yet a peculiar sensation suggested to her that she might want to remain here despite her fear. She desperately longed for answers, and she was sure it would be easier to find them here, but if she let her curiosity rule her head, then she just might find herself stuck here forever. Grace knew that returning home was a case of now or never.

She leapt onto her feet and headed swiftly for the door. She grabbed onto the handle and pulled it fully open. As she bolted back through it, into the darkness, the door shut itself behind her, sealing off her only portal to the ship.

5

"This is a Piccadilly line service to Cockfosters."

If Harriet said it one more time, Grace was going to scream. A group of adolescent boys had sniggered at the announcement for the entire journey on the underground since changing at St Pancras, reminding Grace why she always avoided travelling across London during weekends.

"Who lives in Cockfosters, anyway?"

Grace glanced around her as they crossed over the road. Harriet hadn't exactly made the journey any easier—the two glasses of wine she'd downed before they'd left the house had made her giddy. Grace was just thankful they'd alighted at Wood Green; any longer and she would have cried.

"I don't know anybody who lives there. It's a fun word to say though, isn't it? *Cockfosters. Cock*," she paused for effect, "*fosters*. Hey, maybe tonight we'll get to foster some—"

"Stop it!"

"I was only playing. What's with you today, anyway? You haven't exactly been yourself."

"I'm fine," Grace lied. "I'm just not really in the mood

to face Caroline's idea of entertainment."

"I know she can be a bit—"

"Loud? Chatty? In your face?"

"—excitable; but I don't think she's that bad. We don't need to stay too long if you don't want to. Just a couple of drinks and then we can go."

"I think that's all I can bear! Anyway, there won't be any guys there so you wouldn't be able to foster anything." She forced a smile to keep Harriet happy. She thought it would be best to not bring up the subject of Harriet's on-off relationship with Daniel, and instead assumed Harriet's comment was meant to imply that they were currently very much *off*.

As they turned a corner, Caroline's house came into view at the end of the road. A woman was getting out of her car carrying what appeared to be a Tupperware box.

"Look at how big her—"

"Shh!" Grace nudged Harriet. She *had* noticed the size of the woman's breasts—how could she miss them? - but had made the wise decision not to mention them. She hoped Harriet was going to behave herself tonight; it was never a guarantee when she'd been drinking.

"But they're huge! I bet there are planets smaller than those things!"

Grace swallowed a splutter of laughter, trying to ignore the comment. She tried to change the subject as they neared the house. "Did you remember to pick up the bottle for Caroline?"

She patted her oversized shoulder bag. "Hugging it for safety, you know?"

"Good."

As they turned into the driveway, Caroline's front door flung open. "Gracey, darling!"

"Hi, Caroline." She tried to remember to breathe as Caroline squeezed a hug out of her.

"And Harriet, how lovely to see you again!" It was difficult to tell whether or not she was being sincere.

They'd not been in the same room together for several years, not since Caroline's birthday and the incident with the cute bartender from Manchester. Grace was glad she'd left early that night; the stories she'd heard were painful enough to imagine. She could only be thankful that she hadn't actually witnessed them.

"Take a seat," Caroline said as they headed into the living room. The woman carrying the Tupperware box was sitting in the corner, already nursing a large glass of something fruity and alcoholic. A gaggle of women were clustered around the sofa and sitting on plastic chairs. One blonde woman Grace was sure she'd never met before was slouched in a large beanbag. The air was filled with shrieks of laughter.

"Look what Julie brought!" Caroline pulled the lid off the Tupperware. She thrust it toward Grace and Harriet, who were still standing in the doorway and trying to work out which of the few empty seats they should occupy. Caroline held the Tupperware under their faces to offer them something to nibble on.

"Chocolate penis?"

Grace closed her eyes to wish away her headache. It already seemed like a long night, and they'd only been there just over an hour.

"Carol, where're your cocktail sticks?" a voice called through from the kitchen.

"How do you know I've got any, Nicola?"

"Your kitchen's always loaded!"

Caroline sighed. "Top drawer beneath the knife block," she called. She turned to face the rest of the room. "Right, who's up for a game of Twister?" She pulled out the box from behind her as Julie squealed, "ME!"

"Good heavens!" Grace remarked as she pulled her hand to her ear and leaned toward Harriet to escape the piercing noise.

"I think somebody might have had a bit too much to

drink!" Harriet said. And she was right. Grace was sure that Julie had not had too many drinks, but apparently the few that she'd had were enough to tip her already overly-excitable personality into a state of drunkenness.

As Caroline unfolded the game, even she couldn't deny that perhaps Julie should skip the drinking part of the game as she watched her slump deeper upon the chair on which she was sitting, barely awake.

"So whenever we make a move, we have to drink out of that straw?" asked Laura for confirmation, nodding toward a giant bowl of liquid. It definitely seemed like her idea of a good time.

"Exactly! And whoever is the last one standing on the mat will receive my *special prize*!" Caroline stroked an unmarked package beside her.

"What's in it?"

"Ah now, that would be telling! But let's just say it's very long...and manly...and *very* realistic!" she teased.

Laura, who was pretty sure she knew what it was, clapped her hands enthusiastically. Grace tilted her head back and drained the last of the wine out of her glass.

"Hey, hey, look what I've found!" Nicola was now standing in the doorway of the living room, having returned from the kitchen holding a cocktail sausage in one hand and a packet of balloons in the other.

"Did you enjoy rummaging through my drawers?" asked Caroline, knowing Nicola wouldn't take her remark too seriously.

"Oh, come off it; you love your drawers being rummaged!"

The women on the floor laughed and whistled at Caroline.

"Doesn't she just! How many men has it been now?" asked Megan, who had decided to strap one of the plunge bras from the lingerie box over her t-shirt.

"You be quiet!" Caroline scolded playfully, unable to hide the grin on her face. "And what exactly do you plan on doing with the leftover balloons from my cousin's party?"

"Ooh, ooh, can we blow them up?" pleaded Laura.

Nicola popped the sausage into her mouth and slid into the room, dropping the cocktail stick onto a paper plate on the floor. She took her time opening the packet as she swayed her hips from side to side, offering some unusual balloon-inspired mock strip tease to the rest of the room. She reached into the bag, wiggled her fingers around, and thrust something pink toward the ceiling.

"Do you know what this is?"

"A balloon?" Laura responded, giddily.

"No, my innocent friend, this is not just a balloon!" Nicola drew the opening to her lips and pulled it apart slightly. She began to blow into it, and continued to blow until the limp object had grown into something much longer. Once it was full enough, she tied a knot at the end and balanced it in the palm of her hand.

"Now can you see what it is?"

"It's a penis!" screamed Julie, who seemed to have woken up from her nap at the perfect moment.

"She's right! It is a penis!" Laura continued to clap, her energy ceaseless.

"But it doesn't even look—"

"Oh, come off it, Grace. Stop being such a prude! It's just a bit of fun," remarked Harriet, who leapt to her feet, suddenly enjoying herself.

Caroline grabbed the balloon and held onto it between her legs. She positioned her other hand behind her head and began thrusting her hips back and forth. Her audience erupted in laughter.

"You're so good at that!" Laura squeaked.

Nicola was too busy blowing up a rounded balloon to watch Caroline, and Megan was drawing a nipple onto another balloon with a marker pen. But Grace could see this display perfectly well, and how deeply she wished she couldn't. She just didn't understand it. And where had the wine disappeared to? Her glass was looking sorely empty.

"What are we, ladies?"

Julie burped.

"That's not quite what I was going for, but thank you, Julie!"

"What are we then, Caroline? Tell us, tell us!"

Grace started to wonder whether it was just the endless supply of shots that was making Laura behave like an idiot, or if it was actually the way she always acted. She hoped, for Laura's sake, that it was the former as she watched her jump up and down enthusiastically with no detriment to the flat chest she concealed behind the cartoon mouth that stretched across the petite front of her t-shirt.

"I'll tell you!" Caroline continued. "We, my good friends, are *modern women*!"

More cheers came from the crowd.

"And do you know *why* we're modern women?"

"Why are we modern women, Caroline?" It was Laura again, who, Grace was convinced, had started to believe she was attending a pantomime.

"Because none of us let men tell us what to do! They don't get to boss us around. We don't have to behave like we were put on this earth to do their dirty work! We get to have complete control of our own lives and our own money," she continued thrusting with the balloon, "and you know what the best part is?"

"What?"

"We don't have anything hideous dangling between our legs!"

Grace thought Laura was going to wet herself as she proceeded to roll around on the floor in hysterics. It was definitely time to find the wine.

"Here, let me have a go!" shouted Harriet across the noise, gesturing for Caroline to pass the balloon.

Grace stood up and steadied herself on her feet before thinking about approaching the kitchen to find another bottle.

Just as Caroline launched the object into the air, Grace took a step forward. The phallic balloon skimmed the top of Grace's head as it flew toward Harriet. There was nothing Grace could do but ignore the scene behind her as the balloon began making its way around the room.

As she stood in the kitchen, she poured herself a glass of water and gulped it down. She was hot, dehydrated, and struggling to keep her headache at bay. Her mind was throbbing as she tried to push away the thoughts.

It was no use. Neither silk nightgowns nor adult bunnies were ever going to be enough of a distraction to hold her attention. And she couldn't stop thinking about that letter.

When she'd awoken on the morning of the lingerie party, the autumnal sun had bled through the gap in the curtains, forcing her awake. She'd pulled herself up until she was propped against the pillows, rubbing her head. She'd had the most peculiar dream.

At least, that's what she'd thought it had been.

It was only when she rolled over to check the time, remembering she had a lot to do that day before she and Harriet were due to arrive at Caroline's, that she saw it lying on the bedside table.

The letter was still folded so that her name on the front was facing toward the ceiling. Grace rubbed furiously at her eyes, wishing it to go away. But it was still there when she opened them again. She reached out a trembling hand from under the warmth of the blanket and picked it up. It was just as she remembered it.

Grace did not understand how the letter had made its way into her bedroom. Now that she thought about it, she couldn't remember how she'd gotten into bed. The last thing she could recall was crossing through the door and hearing it bang behind her. She'd been certain it was a dream once she'd woken.

But even if the letter wasn't enough to convince her otherwise, then the metal key sticking out of the door at the top of the landing would have been enough to change her mind. It baffled her to think that she'd never paid any attention to that cupboard before, and that she hadn't even registered that it was there. But as clear as day, she could now see it. Its presence was undeniable. She hadn't been dreaming.

She'd tried to open in again. She needed to see what was on the other side now that it was broad daylight.

She fought but it wouldn't budge. She'd turned the key both ways, jiggled it about in the lock. It was stuck. It was as if somebody, or something, was refusing to allow her to cross back through to wherever it was she'd been the night before.

They certainly wanted her to remember it though. Why else would the letter have mysteriously made its way to her night stand after she'd dropped it in the ship? But the unusual clothes she'd been wearing—the tan bodice and the copper skirt—were nowhere to be seen. She was once again wearing her pink pyjamas with the little clouds. The words inside the letter were her only hope if she was ever going to find out what had happened.

But she didn't read it. It wasn't the case that she didn't *want* to read it. It was just the case that every time she tried to take a moment to sit down and decipher it, something got in the way. When Harriet came up the stairs she'd stuffed the letter away out of sight, as she knew she couldn't risk anybody else finding out about it. And when Harriet walked straight past the door without acknowledging it, it didn't help to reassure Grace that she wasn't just going crazy. She was starting to fear what she didn't understand. Perhaps it would be best if she forgot all about the door and the letter and the ship.

Perhaps if she ignored everything, then maybe it would all go away.

It turned out she was wrong. Her method had lasted until the gathering that evening, but she had to admit the fact that it could be ignored no more. As Caroline entered the kitchen clutching a nurse's outfit made of PVC that she was most definitely going to squeeze into, Grace confirmed to herself that, no matter what happened, she would read that letter tomorrow and find out exactly what was going on. It was the only way her mind would ever be able to rest.

She gulped down another mouthful of water and shuffled her way back into the living room, just in time to see Julie lift up her top and wedge the balloon between her breasts. Maybe the letter wasn't so bad a distraction after all.

6

*F*ran picked at the top of the muffin, flicking the bits of blueberry mindlessly. So far, her morning hadn't been great. The drain in her flat had decided to clog, the fuse had blown on her hair dryer, and just because things always seemed to happen in threes, she'd broken one of her nails when she opened her car door on the way to work. It wouldn't have been so bad if she hadn't just had them manicured. Not even a freshly-baked muffin from the coffee shop down the street was working to cheer her up.

She scrolled through her emails, looking for something to occupy her mind. There were a few messages Grace had forwarded to her, but nothing exciting.

What was Grace's problem, anyway? If Fran decided to walk around in outfits she'd clearly had for what must be at least a decade, she'd probably wish for the ground to swallow her whole. And whatever she did to her hair in the mornings—scraping it back like that—did absolutely nothing to frame her face. She needed layers or something, anything to make her look less plain.

Yes, Fran was most certainly pleased she did not look

like Grace.

But Grace didn't have to spend every single day of her life giving in to Mr Barrie's demands, did she? Grace wasn't the one who was expected to bring his coffee every morning. Grace didn't have to pretend to be grateful for the expensive jewellery he threw her way when really he was bestowing bribes. And it wasn't Grace who had to unfasten the button on his trousers with her teeth when everybody else had left the office to go home. It wasn't Grace's job on the line if she refused to give Mr Barrie exactly what he wanted, was it?

No, *she* didn't have to deal with any of that.

"You're still working on that article about winter footwear, Fran?" Mr Barrie crept up behind her, breaking her concentration

"I've just finished it," she replied, not turning to look at him.

If she had to find the silver lining for her situation, it would be the fact that as long as she concentrated all her energy on giving her boss whatever it was he wanted, she wouldn't have the time to worry about how the rest of her life outside of the office seemed to be spiralling out of her control.

Mr Barrie interrupted her thoughts again. She needed to stop making a habit of drifting off. "I want you to head into town and take a look at the latest bags or accessories or whatever it is you women like to throw yourselves all over this time of year. It's party season, so women are going to need to know what to wear with their little black dresses." He leaned closer to Fran. "There's some money in the top drawer in my office. Pick up something pretty for yourself—maybe go for something that'll accentuate that neckline of yours a little more?" He glanced down, not hiding the fact that he was looking straight down her blouse.

Spending a little time looking around the shops would lift her mood a little—she couldn't deny that—but she wished it was something she could do without having to rely on Mr Barrie's bribery. Giving in to what he desired, she pressed her palms into her back to stretch before standing up and leaning her chest in his direction. Apparently he didn't seem to care that he made her do this right in the middle of the office where everybody could see her. She tried to pretend she didn't care what the others thought, but sometimes she felt like she'd lost all self-respect. But if she wanted to continue to be able to pay her bills and keep a roof over her head, especially now that she was struggling with her imminent divorce, then maybe this was just something she was going to have to live with. With no other alternative in sight, she swallowed her pride and headed for Mr Barrie's office to collect the money.

Mr Barrie scratched at his moustache before turning to face James, who was busy tapping away at his keyboard. "Anything interesting in the news?" He had, of course, read the morning newspapers himself, but he liked to test his employees and put them on the spot. He always gave James half an hour after the daily meeting to go through the newspapers—a generous amount of time as far as Mr Barrie was concerned—before he'd check up on him to make sure that the newest member of his staff was living up to his high standards. Thankfully for James, he always did as he was told.

"Nothing much, sir: another stabbing, gang crime, break-ins. But I still have to go through some of the news sites to see if there's anything breaking. Maybe there's been a murder!"

James had a peculiar appetite for news stories: the more blood and guts, the better. It wasn't that he was malicious, and deep down he hoped that nobody *had* been murdered, but whenever it did happen he tried to think of it like a fictitious story. As long as he maintained the attitude that he was writing a book report for some gripping crime novel, then his emotions wouldn't be affected by the horrors that he had to report on every single day.

"I want you to make some phone calls," Mr Barrie continued, "to see if you can interview somebody involved in anything that's going on. We really need to improve the daily hits on the website...

And Andy," he said, turning in his direction, "you didn't tell me earlier about the match..."

Mr Barrie didn't know the first thing about football, but he certainly liked to pretend that he was interested. Was it not, after all, his duty as a man to love and be devoted to the sport? The last thing he wanted to do was to give the impression that he was soft.

"It was brilliant!" Andy replied. "Both sides played with a lot of energy and enthusiasm. I reckon some of them are going to be fantastic players when they're older."

"Have you put the article online yet?" Andy nodded. "Good. And as I told you earlier, I want you to focus on rugby today. I want who's hot, who's not. A report on the league tables, that sort of thing."

Nobody dared to point out that he didn't have a clue what he was talking about. It wasn't worth the risk to bruise his ego; the consequences for the entire Anchor team would be dire. Grace looked up at Mr Barrie as she fought a never-ending battle with boredom.

"And Grace," he said, "you just carry on doing whatever it is you're doing."

Grace often wondered if Mr Barrie actually knew what he had employed her to do. She may have hated her job, but she respected the fact that, without her there to answer the emails and take phone calls, Mr Barrie would not receive any of the correspondence he needed to sustain the business. And without her there to forward emails to people, nobody would have access to half the stories they produced. She couldn't help but feel undermined.

She slumped lower on her chair. It wasn't even ten o'clock and already she was feeling lethargic. Something told her it was going to be a long day.

With nothing else to do, she pulled up the emails,

hoping there would be something there to keep her mind active for a few minutes. There was one new email. She clicked it open and sighed. She should have known it would be for Fran. She sent it on to Fran's account, knowing all too well that she would love this; she always seemed to enjoy receiving something for nothing, and now Fran was being invited to yet another product launch. She always returned to the office from such events with an entire goody-bag full of new products to review for the website.

No matter how much she disliked Fran though, she had to admit that she was brilliant at networking. If it wasn't for the fact that Mr Barrie kept buttering her up all the time, she probably would have gone elsewhere by now. Grace was certain that Fran was only staying at Anchor because she liked to be flattered by her boss.

Grace tapped in a reply to the sender to inform them that the email had been forwarded to the relevant recipient and that they should expect a response in due course. She didn't need to think about what she was writing, having responded with the exact same message more times than she cared to consider. She sent the email and glanced over to Fran's desk. She watched as she quickly jotted something down in her notebook before standing and putting on her coat. Without looking around the office, she headed straight for the door with what Grace took to be a grin spread across her face.

She looked up at the clock. Five minutes had crawled by since she had last checked the time. She half expected the big hand to start moving backwards soon. Still another six hours and fifty-five minutes until she could go home. No emails to reply to, no queries to answer. What a brilliant start to the week...

There was one positive thing about having nothing else to do though. Glancing around the office, she made sure nobody was watching her. Thankfully everybody was too busy working on their articles to notice her, and Andy, who often wandered over to speak to her, was chewing the end of his pen with his eyes glued to the computer screen, and it didn't look like he'd be moving any time soon. Satisfied that nobody was paying her any attention, she reached under her desk and pulled up her handbag. Unfastening the top, she felt around inside for the pocket at the back.

It was still there.

She held the letter in her hands and read her name on the front: *Miss Grace Byrne.*

She inhaled deeply, preparing herself for the one thing she'd been putting off all weekend. It was time to read the letter.

> *Dear Miss Byrne,*
>
> *I made the decision to leave this letter inside one of my boots as I knew you would be requiring them. I hope they fit you reasonably well. I expect you have a lot of questions you would like to ask me. However, I am afraid that I am unable to answer them for you at this moment. The answers to your questions are something that you must, and will, discover for yourself as you travel through your journey. I ask only that you trust your instincts. I know you will do the right thing. And remember, a walk in my boots will help you see that there isn't anything you can't be.*
>
> *Your friend,*
> *Gráinne*

If Grace had expected that reading the letter would help to clear her mind, she had been wrong. It was written in dark ink, the words formed from the tip of a quill. Some of the letters were difficult to read, but she had managed to make her way down the scroll until she reached the end.

Gráinne? She didn't know anybody by that name. There had once been a Gráinne living on her street when she was a child, but that didn't seem to be a likely connection. She scanned the letter again.

"A walk in my boots will help you see," she whispered under her breath so that nobody could hear her muttering the words to herself, "that there isn't anything you can't be."

What was that supposed to mean? Grace was no longer thinking about how the letter had come into her possession; it was more important now that she concentrated on whatever it was the letter was trying to tell her.

It had to be some sort of a riddle. She thought about how she'd found the note inside the pair of boots on the ship. Boots which she had now learned belonged to somebody named Gráinne.

Grace had often heard about weird mystery trails around the world. Not the fun kind like hunting for Easter eggs in the garden, but scavenger hunts conducted by anonymous communities online. It wasn't territory she particularly wished to involve herself in as she knew how nasty it could get, but there was a possibility that somebody on the Internet had concocted this riddle. It wouldn't help her understand how she'd apparently managed to be transported back a few centuries, but maybe it would at least help her solve the problem that lay directly in front of her.

She typed in the words into a search bar and hit the enter key. The screen flashed as it brought up pages of results. After a few seconds though, Grace realised that none of them seemed to be what she was looking for. They were all concerned with selling self-help books or offering cheap hiking trips up and down the country. There were no matches for the words of the letter.

Grace folded it up neatly and placed it into the pouch in her bag, out of sight. She tried to replay the entire event in her mind, searching for things that might give her clues. But it was hopeless. She wasn't getting anywhere.

But then she remembered something. *Didn't the ship have something written on its side? A name of some sort?* She thought for a moment, rubbing the tips of her fingers against the sides of her head as if trying to help the information come forth.

"The Pirate Queen!" She flung a hand to her mouth, worried she'd said it too loudly. She glanced around. Nobody was looking at her.

Grace searched for the name and waited for the results to load. She clicked on the first link and started reading.

She had hoped to find photographs of the ship so she could confirm that it was the same one, but she soon realised why she wasn't finding anything. According to the website, *The Pirate Queen* was associated with the sixteenth century—or more accurately, sixteenth-century Ireland.

"So I was in Ireland?" Grace said to herself, a little more quietly this time.

"Wait... She was a person?"

It hadn't been quite what she had expected to read, but something inside her told her that this was exactly what she was looking for. She continued down the page, muttering to herself as she read out loud to help her take in the information.

"So, *The Pirate Queen* is the name given to an Irish pirate," she confirmed to herself: "Grace O'Malley, better known to those in Ireland as Gráinne, or Granuaile." She stumbled over the last word, butchering the pronunciation. It took a few seconds for the information to register before Grace realised exactly what it was that she had discovered.

"*Grace* O'Malley!" she gasped as she finally took it in. Why hadn't it occurred to her immediately that her own name was the Anglicisation of Gráinne? She was starting to think she hadn't spent nearly enough time researching her heritage.

Her head was starting to spin. "The girl, Cathleen, what was it she'd called me?' She tried to think back, but her mind was racing so fast that she was struggling to digest the information. She looked at the screen again and as she read the words and it all started coming back to her. "Miss *something*, wasn't it? Miss...Granuaile? That's it! Miss Granuaile!" She absorbed the word on the screen as she rejoiced in remembering the name, pronouncing it more accurately this time. "Cathleen must have thought that I was Grace O'Malley!"

This new information was a welcomed relief, but still little of it made sense to Grace. How could she find herself in sixteenth-century Ireland, being mistaken for a pirate she had never heard of before and with whom she shared a first name?

Okay, so she'd established that the boots in the ship—the boots in which she'd first discovered her letter—belonged to Gráinne O'Malley. Perhaps the clothes Grace had somehow found herself wearing had been Gráinne's too. But it still didn't explain much. Grace hadn't even heard of this pirate woman before, so why was she trying to communicate with her? And *how* was she doing it? She couldn't possibly know about Grace four hundred years before she was even born.

She continued reading down the page. 'Grace O'Malley's castle on Clare Island still stands today.' Next to the paragraph there was a small photograph of a grey building. It took a moment for it to register with Grace before she realised that it was the same castle she'd seen in the distance when she had climbed down from the ship.

She was about to continue down the page when the phone on her desk rang.

"Anchor News; Grace speaking," she said as she picked up the receiver. *Typical*, she thought: *Nobody ever rings except when I'm in the middle of something important.* "Sure, I'll put you through to him."

Catching Andy's eye to alert him of the incoming call,

she transferred it to his desk and put down the phone.

She turned her attention back to her monitor, but before she had a chance to read any further she noticed Andy coming toward her. She quickly closed down the web page that was open in front of her and pulled up the Anchor homepage.

"Cheese and onion or chicken and mayo?" He stood at her desk and produced two takeaway sandwiches.

"Ooh, cheese and onion, please!" She took the lunch gratefully and tore open the plastic wrap. She'd been running late as usual and hadn't had time for breakfast, something of which her rumbling stomach had reminded her all morning.

"Working hard, are we?" Andy teased as he ripped into his own sandwich and took a bite.

"As ever..." She rolled her eyes at him. "Quick phone call, was it?"

"Yeah, it wasn't anything important. I'd just asked for some information confirmation and they said they'd get back to me."

"Which they did..."

"Yes, which they did. So, how much fun has your day been?"

"Oh, enthralling!" She raised her thumbs in the air, adding to her sarcasm.

"Well, why don't I give you something to look forward to?" he said.

"What do you have in mind?"

"It depends! Do you have plans for this evening?"

Grace pretended to think for a moment, not wanting to confess that she rarely made plans to do anything that didn't involve takeaway food and a night in front of the television. "I can't say that I do," she finally replied.

"Good. Look, if I'm honest, I'm in need of a favour from you."

"Ah, so that's what the sandwiches are for," Grace baited.

"Pretty much..."' Which they both knew wasn't true as Andy would often pick up something for her if he had time. Last week it had been a Twix and a can of Diet Coke, both received as warmly as the sandwich. "My sister's got this thing tonight—a function of some sort—and she wants me to watch Mollie, my niece." Was Andy stumbling with his words? "I said I'd take her out for something to eat, but I'm really not that good with kids. I don't suppose you'd want to join me?"

"Sure."

"I promise she's as good as gold, never saying much and always remembering her manners—"

"Andy, I said I'll come with you!"

"—oh, thank you, Grace. You're a life-saver, you really are. We can head there straight after work. Sarah's dropping her off around half five. Right, I'm just popping out for a bit. I'll be back though, don't worry!" Andy winked before turning round, dropping his now empty sandwich packet into the nearby bin, and heading out of the door.

So it's not exactly a date he's after, but...

If only for that moment, Grace forgot all about Ireland and Gráinne and the letter that she'd managed to return to her bag before anyone had seen it. There was something about Andy she'd found particularly alluring ever since she'd joined the Anchor team. They had a great working relationship—a friendship, Grace hoped - but they'd not really had the chance to spend time together outside of work.

Perhaps this was going to be the start of something beautiful. It didn't matter to Grace that his niece was going to be there too. She felt like a teenager again as she thought about seeing him after office hours. She tried not to squeal as she struggled to contain herself. At long last she was going to spend some time with him, and only that time would tell where their relationship would lead to after that. As her imagination conjured some of her wildest fantasies, she blushed.

The rest of the day crawled by much more slowly than usual. For once, though, Grace was thankful for the lack of work to do. After forcing her wandering mind through the rest of the article about Grace O'Malley that she'd been in the middle of before Andy had come over to her, she allowed herself to slip into a daydream, leaving her unable to concentrate on anything except the possible events of that evening that were slowly unravelling inside her mind.

She kept playing it over and over again in her head, imagining conversations she'd share with Andy. She thought about what he might order, what she might eat; it didn't matter that he hadn't actually told her where they were going. Perhaps they'd go somewhere for Thai food. Or maybe they'd visit an Italian restaurant, and they could share a plate of spaghetti. Then they would each take an end of a ribbon of pasta and bite their way down towards the middle until their lips met...all with the child sitting right next to them.

Grace was forced out of her daydream when Andy arrived back at the office to pick her up. "Back just in time. Didn't I promise?" he grinned.

He had tapped Grace on the shoulder to get her attention, causing her to nearly jump right out of her seat. Everybody else had already gone home, except Mr Barrie and Fran, who were both in the boss's office doing whatever it was they did when they were alone. Grace didn't know the details but she was certain she never wanted to find out.

"Are you ready then?" Andy asked.

As ready as I'll ever be, Grace thought to herself as she shut down the computer, forcing herself to hide the excitement that was rapidly building inside her.

As they headed down Regent Street, butterflies fluttering in her stomach, Andy still hadn't said where they were going. Too impatient to wait any longer, Grace finally asked.

"It's this great little diner just round the corner on Charing Cross Road. I've been there a few times with Mollie and she really seems to enjoy it, so I thought we'd play it safe and stick to somewhere she knows. She's not the easiest to please with food!"

"I've never been in a diner before," Grace confessed.

"Well you're going to love it. It's very retro."

When they reached the entrance, she agreed that it looked spectacular. For some reason she couldn't remember ever having seen this one before; maybe it was just because she hadn't ever sought it out. There were lots of independent restaurants and diners around London but the ones Grace usually noticed were sleek with posh fonts and fancy lettering. Not this one though. Both the front window and the frame of the door were decorated with bright neon lights, lit up in different colours: blues, greens, yellows, reds. The display was alluring, stunning. It was unique, and that was something Grace admired.

They stopped and turned their backs on the diner to face the street. "Sarah shouldn't be too long. I must warn you though, she's a bit—"

The BMW pulled up in front of them: shiny new paintwork, chrome finishes, clearly worth not a penny lower than Grace's annual salary.

"—flash."

He wasn't kidding either. The tall woman slid out of the driver's seat. Her cream suit highlighted her slim figure, her large sunglasses drawing attention to her bronzed cheekbones. A blonde ponytail swished around her waist, tied up tightly to match the rest of her immaculate image.

Andy hugged his sister with a distinct lack of any real embrace.

She opened the side door and out stepped Andy's petite niece: soft brown curls, pale skin, rosy cheeks. Her eyes were wide as her eyelashes were long. Between her natural features and her little red woollen duffel coat that would do any Edwardian child proud, she remarkably resembled a little porcelain doll.

"I'll pick Mollie up from your place at around ten, if that's okay with you?"

"Sure. Hello, Mollie." He bent down and hugged the child.

"Hi, Uncle Andy." Her whisper was barely audible, her voice a delicate product of her sheltered life.

"Mollie, this is Grace, a friend of mine." He gestured toward her as she stood back on the pavement, shifting her feet awkwardly.

"Hello." Grace decided to add a small wave for effect. The child smiled slightly but didn't speak.

"As I said," Andy spoke to Grace from the side of his mouth, "she's quite shy. Don't take it personally."

"Right, give mummy a kiss." Sarah leaned forward so Mollie could kiss her cheek. "Have fun with Uncle Andy."

And without another word, she drove off.

Once they were inside the diner, Grace was just as amazed as she had been by the exterior. An assortment of tables was arranged around the diner floor. Some were circular with individual seats in an open space. Others resembled little booths to allow for a more intimate experience. She was equally surprised and delighted to discover that Andy had selected a booth for them.

Grace took in the surroundings as they waited for their order. "It's very nice in here. Quite American, isn't it?"

"Oh, it's lovely. I've been here quite a few times, and it's always such an inviting place. In the evenings they play music on that jukebox over there." He pointed to the corner of the room near the toilets. "It can actually get quite lively in here, believe it or not! I only tend to come in when I'm looking after Mollie, of course." She was sitting next to him, concentrating on the picture she was colouring that had been provided by the diner. "I'll have an occasional something to eat here myself after work though and catch up with a few newspapers if I've been out all day. It's a nice place to relax and escape from the cold. I suppose I should probably endeavour to be a bit more adventurous with what I eat here though. I always order the same thing! I did try their veggie burger once, actually. It was quite nice. I could never give up real burgers though!"

"Neither could I."

"You'll love the cheeseburger. The first time I took a bite out of one of those beauties I thought I'd died and gone to heaven."

The waitress who had taken their order approached the table, carrying two trays. She was younger than Grace, in her early twenties perhaps, and wore her blonde hair in short plaits at either side of her face. Around her waist she'd wrapped a green apron, with a cap of the same colour resting on the top of her head.

"Three cheeseburgers and fries with chocolate milkshakes?"

"Yes, that's us." Andy replied. "Thank you."

The waitress unloaded the trays. "Enjoy your meal," she said before heading off to take another order. Mollie didn't hesitate as she began tucking into her chips, probably thankful for another excuse not to have to talk or interact with anybody.

Grace looked down at her own plate. She couldn't believe the size of the cheeseburger. The hearty helping was wedged in between two thick slices of bun, the melted cheese oozing and bubbling hot in the middle. A fair display of chips—sorry, *fries*—lay at the side of it. Grace was sure they were the longest fries she'd ever seen. The milkshake had arrived in a tall glass, its look finished off with a pink straw. Andy had been given a green straw, Grace noticed. She started to wonder what Andy's favourite colour was. She decided he looked like he'd enjoy blue, or perhaps orange, and made a mental note to find out.

"It smells amazing, doesn't it?"

"I don't know where to begin!"

Andy laughed and reached for the plastic basket of condiments on the table. "Now call me disgusting, but I have to have mustard with my chips. I'm afraid it's one of my greatest weaknesses." He pulled out the yellow bottle and gave it a shake before turning it upside down and squeezing a dollop of mustard onto the side of his plate.

"I think I'll stick with plain old ketchup. I don't think my culinary adventures would stretch as far as yours." She squeezed the red bottle so that her fries were decorated in the sauce. She reached for her cutlery and separated the knife and fork from the paper napkin.

"Mollie doesn't like any sauce, do you?" She shook her head and popped another chip into her mouth. "Anyway, I wouldn't say I'm overly adventurous myself," he laughed. "I'm sitting in a backstreet diner with a burger the size of a house in front of me. I'm not really one for fancy restaurants. You know the sort where you end up paying an entire month's wages for little more than a raisin in the middle of the plate? I know some consider it to be an art form, but I just don't care for all that intricate presentation stuff. No, I like my food to be something tasty that will fill me up."

"I couldn't agree more."

"Ah yes, just as I remembered it!" Andy remarked as he shovelled a fork of burger into his mouth, having cut it into portions. "I've not been here in at least a month. I swear I was starting to get withdrawal symptoms!"

Grace cut a piece of the cheeseburger and popped it into her mouth. As she chewed, she began to realise exactly what Andy had been talking about. The burger was juicy and not overdone, but not so soft that it turned the crispy bun soggy. The cheese was wonderful and creamy. She couldn't believe she'd never heard of this place. Now that she thought about it, she couldn't recall seeing a name above the door.

"Wow! You were right. It's delicious!" She picked up

her milkshake and drew the straw to her lips. As she sucked, her mouth was overcome with the sweet chocolate taste. It was thick, but not lumpy: just the way Grace thought it should be. "I don't think I've had a chocolate milkshake since I was a teenager!"

"They're amazing, aren't they? I know they're a little naughty, but it's such a wonderful indulgence. All in moderation, as I keep reminding myself, or I'll end up needing a new wardrobe." He tugged at his jacket.

Grace smiled, thinking to herself how dapper Andy looked. He was always smartly dressed in his suits and ties for work. She wondered what he liked to wear during weekends when he was away from the office.

"I've been craving this since this morning. It definitely hits the spot after a long day."

"I know how you feel!"

"Don't get me wrong; I love working away from the office. But it's November, and even with a scarf around my neck, it's still freezing! I just keep reminding myself that it'll be tennis season soon enough."

"Do you play tennis?"

"Occasionally; I used to play for the school team, and I used to compete in regional competitions."

"Wow!"

"I loved mixed doubles. I think I won most of my matches that way. I don't really have the time for it now, so I only play now and then. What about you? Do you play any sports?"

Grace snorted, narrowly avoiding bringing milkshake down her nose.

"I'll take that as a no then!"

"It's just not something I was ever good at. I hated gym lessons at school, and I think my opinions about sports have remained the same from there. I did go to gymnastics for a while in primary school, but I think that's something every little girl tries. But all in all, I wasn't particularly enthusiastic about it."

"I love writing about sport, but it's not the same as actually taking part. I suppose it's not for everybody. But more importantly, how's the job going?" he asked as he piled a few fries onto his fork.

The look on Grace's face said it all.

"Still not enjoying it?"

"I wish I could say that I was. If Mr Barrie would give me something more to do, then maybe it wouldn't be so bad. It becomes so tedious after the first five minutes of responding to emails. I spend half the day praying for the phone to ring just so I have somebody to talk to for a few minutes. But it's not as if we're flooded with queries every day. Well, apart from those for Fran. She seems to receive no end to requests for freebies, I swear!"

"Yeah, Fran seems to be good at—"

"Sucking up?"

"You say sucking *up*, but I was thinking more along the lines of sucking—" He glanced at Mollie, suddenly reminded of her presence. "—something else. She certainly knows how to get what she wants."

"She's got the boss wrapped around her little finger."

"Are you sure her little finger's not wrapped around the boss?" Andy winked.

Her sudden laughter caused her to squeak. She threw her hand in front of her mouth to try and control herself. "I'm glad I'm not the only one who sees what's going on between those two," she finally managed.

"They don't exactly conceal it. I dread to think what they were up to when we left this evening. Honestly, whenever I'm called into the boss's office for whatever reason, I always wince when I have to sit down in that chair."

The image was too much to bear. Grace couldn't believe how relaxed she felt. She had been so worried that she would become rigid with nerves, but she realised now that it was silly of her to be concerned about such a thing. She always enjoyed Andy's company, and he was never dull to talk to. She felt like a giddy schoolgirl again, drinking milkshakes and giggling over inappropriate conversations with a friend.

She thought for a moment about that word: *friend*. She wanted to ask Andy why he'd brought her here. Sure, he'd said he needed company while he watched Mollie, but hadn't he also said that this wasn't the first time he'd been here with her? Why was he asking Grace along *now*? She'd worked with him for several years but they'd never shared personal time together. Andy broke the interlude.

"Not that I'm trying to get rid of you or anything, but have you thought about looking for another job?"

That certainly wasn't what Grace had expected him to come out with. "To be honest, I've not really given it much thought. I'm quite comfortable at Anchor—at least, I have you for company, and James—and to be honest, I'm not sure I'm ready to move on yet. I was hoping I'd be able to make something more of this job. If only I could find a way!"

"Well, I'm sure you'll think of something."

"I had an interesting conversation with Fran yesterday."

Why had she said that? What good was it going to do to bring this up now?

"Fran? Really?"

"Yeah, she was smoking outside as I was leaving the building. She suggested that I need to try harder if I wanted to get anywhere—something about using my charms as a woman or something. I did consider what she'd said, but I don't really believe in pretending to be somebody I'm not. I just can't do it."

"Too right, Grace. She had no business telling you what you should and shouldn't do. Nobody should have to act falsely just to gain an increase at the workplace. You're beautiful just the way you are; don't let anybody tell you otherwise."

"Thanks, Andy. You know, I think I needed to hear that," Grace said as she tried not to blush. You're probably right; I *should* start looking for another job if Mr Barrie is going to leave me in this dead end. But I just wish I could find a way to convince him that I'm capable of more."

"Then why don't you give yourself a deadline?"

"A deadline?"

"Yeah! If you're still unhappy by, let's say, January, then perhaps it's time to start looking for somewhere else. You're talented and you've got plenty of transferable skills, so I'm sure you'd find something suitable. You're clearly not fulfilled in your current job; perhaps a change would do you good. I want you to promise me that you'll do that."

She thought about it. "Maybe that is a good idea. It's probably for the best. Okay, I'll do it. If I haven't found a way to convince Mr Barrie to increase my responsibilities by January, then I'll start searching for something different."

"Promise?"

"I promise!" She was smiling at Andy, but on the inside Grace couldn't quite believe what she was saying. Was she really ready to leave Anchor? She certainly wasn't ready to say goodbye to Andy. But unless she wanted to go back on her word, she'd have to come up with a way to convince Mr Barrie to give her more to do, and fast.

As she chewed on another forkful of fries, she was certain she could hear the clock ticking away inside her head, counting down the seconds until her life would change forever.

7

*H*e tried to prevent himself from stumbling as the stout figure forced him through the archway, but it had been no use. He tripped to one side, smacking his entire weight against the wall. He slumped to the floor, thankful at least that he hadn't fallen to the ground. The chains around his wrists grew tighter every time he moved; he had only just been able to stop his face from smashing against the floor without the iron cutting deeply into him.

They reached the top of the staircase. Lord Bingham gripped the back of the young man's shirt with one hand and fumbled for a key with the other. He found what he was looking for, clutched it tightly, and turned to his prisoner.

"By the order of Her Majesty Queen Elizabeth, you are to remain locked up until Her Majesty has delivered your fate." The stench of port was strong on his breath as he snarled, moving closer to the man's face. "If I catch you so much as thinking about escaping, you'll regret the day you ever messed with me."

The glee on Bingham's face was as evident now as it had been when he had triumphed over the Irish at

Burrishoole. Tibbott had been certain he would be invincible. There had been a plan devised, and he was sure it was finally going to be the key to victory. The men had been assembled and they were ready to take action.

But perhaps he hadn't thought it through properly. Their strategy had been formed in haste. Why he ever thought the small cluster of fighters he'd gathered would have been enough to overthrow Bingham, he wasn't certain. He had declared that nothing would be able to stop him, but he had spoken too soon.

He only had himself to blame for his capture.

Bingham flung him through the open door and into the tiny room, his eyes flaring with a thirst for revenge. Tibbott fell backward, banging his head against the wall. His clothes seemed to instantly attract the thick dust that coated the floor, accentuated as the narrow window out of reach at the top cast a sickly beam of sunlight onto his torn shirt. He lifted his hand to the back of his head. There was no sign of blood. He would be okay.

"Good morrow, *sir*," Lord Bingham grinned as he banged the metal door shut before skipping down the flight of stairs, abandoning Tibbott Bourke to his suffering.

Her Majesty would be pleased with him. He could feel it in his bones as he rubbed his hands together excitedly, satisfied with his triumph over that vermin Irish boy. Soon rewards would be bestowed on him for bringing the boy to her, and he would stand proudly in Her Majesty's favour. This was his chance to prove his worth to her, and nothing was going to ruin it for him now.

8

"To be honest, Grace, I haven't been to see anything in quite a while. In fact, the last time I went to the cinema would have been..." Andy thought to himself for a moment. "You know something? I don't think I've been since I was a teenager."

"Seriously?"

"Shocking, I know! And it was expensive to go then; I dread to think how much it costs now. I expect I'd need to take out a mortgage just to buy a box of popcorn!" He held the door open as they left the diner. They'd finished complaining about work and had spent the rest of the evening discussing the more relaxing things in life: trashy television, feel-good music, and the latest comedies.

"Thanks," she commented, walking under his arm and onto the street after Mollie had scuttled out. She buttoned her coat to avoid the harsh, biting wind.

"Which is the most convenient Tube station for you from here?"

"Leicester Square will be fine. I can get the Northern line from there."

"We'll walk with you then, won't we Mollie?" The child

71

nodded, her attention fixed upon the cracks in the pavement as she tried to avoid stepping on them. They dawdled in the direction of the station.

"I loved popcorn as a child," Grace continued the conversation, praying they wouldn't run out of things to say to each other. "I probably wouldn't care too much for it now though. Mind you, I shouldn't wish for anything to eat right now anyway. I'm truly stuffed after that meal!"

"Me too! But wasn't I right? Aren't those burgers the most amazing things in the world?"

"I can't argue with that! My sweet tooth will be craving that chocolate milkshake for the next two weeks."

"I know what you mean. I do try to cut down on my visits to the diner now. I fear my waist line will start to protest otherwise. But it's quite a challenge when the food's as good as that."

Grace could see the sign for the underground up ahead as they approached the station. More than anything, she didn't want the evening to end. She'd still not been able to find out whether or not Andy had an ulterior motive in asking her out to dinner.

"Here we are. Your chariot awaits, Miss Byrne." He bowed to Grace as they reached the entrance to the station. She started to wish she *could* ride in a chariot instead of being stuck in the rush hour nightmare. Perhaps she and Andy could have a beautiful *Cinderella* carriage with white horses to take them around as they gazed up at the stars while in each other's arms. And maybe her Fairy Godmother could wave her magic wand to persuade Mr Barrie to enhance her position within the company.

And maybe pigs will fly...

She giggled at Andy as he straightened up, her attention drifting back to her immediate surroundings as she allowed her fantasising to escape her. This was a new side to Andy she'd never seen before. Perhaps he was just trying to entertain Mollie, but something told Grace that this charismatic character before her was the real Andy.

"Thank you, kind sir," she replied accordingly. "I have had a most wonderful evening. I dare say it has been spectacular!"

"It has been my pleasure, I assure you. It was nice to have some company, wasn't it, Mollie?" The child looked up but remained habitually silent.

"And thank you for paying. You really didn't have to do that."

"I know I didn't *have* to. But I wanted to, Grace."

He caught her eye as she looked fondly at him. If there was ever a perfect moment to kiss someone for the first time, this was it. But he wasn't going to do it with his young niece watching, was he?

"Well, you'll have to come over to my place sometime so we're even. Perhaps you'll allow me to cook something for you to say thank you for listening to my endless worries about the office."

Did she just invite Andy over to her house? The words had left her mouth quicker than she'd had time to think about them.

"Grace, you don't need to thank me for listening to you; I'd always help you out however I can. But I'd love to come over." Mollie released a tired yawn beside him. "I'd better get this one back to my place before she falls asleep. Will you be okay from here?"

"Of course."

"I guess I'll see you tomorrow then. Goodnight, Grace." Andy smiled at her and lifted his hand in the air to wave as he carted Mollie away from the station's entrance. As they made their way down the road, Grace remained rooted to the spot where she stood.

It wasn't the goodbye she'd hoped for. She started to wonder whether or not it had been foolish of her to even think that he could possibly wish for anything more than friendship from her. But the young girl was with him, and he definitely wouldn't have made a move with her around. It was impossible to tell how he felt about her.

But Andy had agreed to go to her house for a meal. Surely, if he only considered her to be a friend, then he wouldn't think about crossing that boundary. It would be just the two of them. It would be intimate. It was unlikely that he would have shown an interest in attending such a private engagement if he wasn't a little curious to discover her on a more personal level.

She turned away from the entrance and headed toward the escalators. Andy may have escaped from her sight but he still remained in her mind as she descended toward the platform. He would continue to occupy her thoughts for the entire journey home. He remained there as she walked toward Haverstock Hill, and still he resided in her mind as she entered her house. She couldn't deny it any longer. She was desperately and painfully smitten with Andy.

There was nothing peculiar about the house when Grace returned. It stood in the same spot in the same street, its walls darkened by the blackness of the evening. The inside of the house was as Grace had always known it: a slight draft from a dodgy window, the faint murmuring from the pipes when she clicked the heating on, the weird smell of musk she could never seem to remove from the old building.

It had been three days since she'd found herself on the other side of the cupboard. Although it had occupied her mind throughout the day, she hadn't thought about it at all during her evening with Andy.

Harriet was out for the evening, so she decided to wind down with a more relaxed night to calm her thoughts. She boiled the kettle, poured the water into her mug, and drained the teabag. She flicked through the TV, sighing at the repeats on every channel. She leafed through a magazine that Harriet had left on the coffee table: stilettos, mascara, cellulite. She returned her mug to the kitchen, said goodnight to Bella, who was curled up on the sofa. She locked the front door and headed for the stairs.

The ascent was nothing unusual. It was a journey Grace found neither pleasant nor disturbing. It was only when she reached the top of the stairs that she began to feel a little queasy.

She noticed it as soon as she reached the landing. She couldn't have missed it. The events from the Friday previous came storming to the front of her mind as she stared at the cupboard door. It looked exactly the same, with the key still sticking out of the keyhole where she had left it. However, there was something different this time.

It was open.

The door stood ajar, and from the gap where it had opened, a faint light tickled at the darkness of the landing. It was soft, but it was distinct. She took a step closer. Hesitant, she held out her left hand and placed it on the doorknob. It wasn't as cold as she'd remembered it, but she could still feel the same breeze drifting out from the bottom of the door.

For the first time since that afternoon she thought back to her research from earlier in the day. It had helped her to understand where she'd been, but she still had so many questions that remained unanswered. She knew deep down that she couldn't refuse the door. It must be open for a reason.

I must go back.

She pulled the door back so that there was an entrance big enough for her to fit through. The light still glowed gently as it beckoned her forward. She held her breath, her nerves creeping to the surface. This was something she had to do. She needed to be brave. She inhaled through her nostrils and counted.

One...

Two...

Three...

Grace stepped into the cupboard and the door clicked shut behind her.

The room was just as she'd left it. The bed looked as if

it hadn't been slept in. The candle still stood at the centre of the floor. She walked over to it and picked it up. Grace was sure the wax hadn't melted at all since her first visit—how many days had passed in this world since then? She had no idea whether or not time would operate in the same way here. Perhaps she had just entered through the cupboard at the exact moment at which she had left it. It was impossible to tell from inside the ship.

She held the candle out with her arm stretched so that the glow from the flame circled round her. She looked down at herself and studied her outfit. She was wearing the same clothes as last time: the chemise with the sleeves reaching down to her wrists, the bodice tied with the black string. The skirt still flowed around her ankles, the fabric brushing against her feet, which, once again, were bare. She noticed this time that her hair had changed too. Instead of being tied up in a bun just as she'd fixed it for work, it now stretched right down her back. She'd apparently forgotten how long she'd had let it grow out as she rarely let it down. But now it was free, reaching just above her waist, tints of red shimmering within the brown locks as the light of the candle occasionally reached it.

Grace stood for a moment, the candlestick still in her hand, as she tried to decide what to do next. She acknowledged that a few things were different this time: she knew where she was now; she knew what was outside. But she still didn't know why. She would find that out eventually, she was sure of it. She just had to work a little harder. She glanced around the room searching for her next move.

It was then that the boots caught her attention. They were exactly where she had left them, lying in front of the chest, one standing upright and the other resting on its side from when she'd dropped it in her hurry to escape. As she stared at them, the words inside the letter came flooding back to her.

"A walk in my boots will help you see," Grace uttered

the first line out loud, her eyes still fixed on the footwear, "that there isn't anything that you can't be."

If she had hoped that saying it out loud would make it easier to unravel this riddle, she remained disappointed. She still didn't understand. "But what am I supposed to be? I'm not even sure who I am anymore."

The confusion had started to build again until a thought that she knew wasn't her own pushed its way to the front of her mind.

Don't think, Grace. Just act.

Her eyes flicked back and forth as she acknowledged the voice inside her head. What was it she had to do?

And then it hit her. She had to put the boots on. She approached them and lowered herself down to the ground so that she could place the candlestick beside the chest. There was nothing for her to sit on or rest herself against to stop her from stumbling over, so there was only one other option: she sat herself down firmly on the floor. It took her a moment to adjust to the new contact with the room; she was now leaving herself vulnerable to any sudden invasions. In the time it would take for her to stand back up and reach for the door to flee, an attacker could conceivably kill her. But she knew worrying wasn't really an option. She had instructions to follow.

She pulled her foot closer to her as she picked up the right boot: the one in which she'd found the letter. Between her fingers the material felt thin. They were still quite tough—they weren't old or worn away—but they didn't look or feel as sturdy or as protective as she had expected for a pair of leather boots. Inhaling deeply, she moved her foot so that she could slide it inside the boot. Why placing on a pair of boots was such a strenuous ordeal she didn't know, but something told her that this was important.

She moved slowly as her toes made their way down the opening. The top was tall and narrow. She felt it make its way up her bare leg as her foot worked its way toward the sole. Finally, she felt her toes reach the front of the boot. She wiggled them to ensure her foot was firmly in place.

She pulled the left boot on, much quicker this time now that she was comfortable that there'd be no more unexpected items hidden at the bottom. The top of the boots were folded over—they were surprisingly similar, she thought, to the traditional footwear she had seen as a child when she went to see *Peter Pan* on stage during pantomime season.

Grace placed a hand on the chest and pushed her weight upon it to help her stand. The boots were neither too tight nor too loose. They were a perfect fit.

It occurred to Grace that any fears she had previously felt, any anxieties that had hit her upon entering these surroundings again, had disappeared. She took in the room again, casting her eyes around her. Everything felt so familiar now. The air wasn't as cold as she'd remembered it either. And it wasn't just the room that felt different.

A peculiar sensation washed over Grace. At first she couldn't quite put her finger on it, but she suddenly started to feel—how could she put it?—experienced. There was something about her mind that began to feel like it had been fed decades of adventures in a matter of minutes. Grace wasn't sure what they were exactly, as she struggled to locate anything specific, but she certainly *felt* like she'd seen the world. Although the nerves hadn't completely left her, she felt stronger, mentally ready to take on anything life threw at her. Even if she wasn't sure whose life she was living.

Taking a moment to consider her next move, she blushed as she recalled her earlier haste to evacuate. It seemed so bizarre now that she would have wished so eagerly to leave. She was no longer a stranger to the ship. There was nothing stopping her now. She headed for the door in front of her and pulled it open. Unlike her previous visit, however, there was no burst of sunlight to welcome her. The sky had darkened as the day had aged.

Undeterred, Grace stormed out onto the ship's deck.

"I thought as much. You're rarely away from it.' He managed half a smile, trying not to let her see the panic on his face. But he had to tell her. "You must come with me immediately. They've got your son, Gráinne. They've caught Tibbott!"

9

The clock chimed and Elizabeth straightened herself in the seat as she made herself more comfortable. It was rare that she had a morning to herself, and she planned to make the most of this occasion. She was always busy, yet she was consistently bored. Perhaps today she could go for a stroll in the grounds or take up some activity to occupy her mind.

"Maybe I'm just going too soft in my old age," she mumbled to herself. How much posset had she had to drink last night? Her health had not been great recently. "The years have been good to me, but what would my mother think?" The mother she had outlived. The mother she had never known.

Her Tudor blood still ran thick through her veins. She wouldn't allow anybody to tell her any different. Not that they'd try to for fear of being struck down. "Would he be proud?" she sighed as she wondered of her father. Had she grown into the Queen he would have wanted her to be? She could only hope that she would have satisfied her parents. She had done all that her strength would allow, that much she knew.

She shifted her body to face the window. Fixing her attention on the river below, she lost herself in the quiet.

Nothing could have dampened Lord Bingham's mood that day. Her Majesty would be so pleased with him, he could feel it. He'd hardly slept all night, too excited to tell her the wonderful news. He could almost taste his reward.

He'd allowed Her Majesty time to stir from her bedchambers but once the clock had struck nine, he found that he could not wait any longer. He had to steady himself as he skipped along the corridor, not wanting anybody to see him so inappropriately merry.

He came to a halt outside the room in which Her Majesty was sitting so that he could compose himself. After straightening out his jacket he stood for a moment, watching her through the gap in the door. She was resting in her chair, one foot crossed over the other. Not prepared for visitors that morning, she was dressed more plainly than usual in a slender dress of red silk. Lord Bingham admired her fiery hair, which had been neatly arranged on her head. She was beautiful. If only she would notice him, think of him as more than a humble devotee.

He sighed to himself, then coughed: "Your Majesty?"

She jumped, startled by the intrusion. "Lord Bingham. You have returned from Ireland. What is it?" She made sure there was a level of anger in her voice to assert her authority over the disruption, but she would secretly confess to herself that she was glad for the company, as the boredom to which she was so accustomed had once again started to develop. She was beginning to grow weary.

Lord Bingham entered the room as Elizabeth stood up.

"Your Majesty, I bring you good news," he spoke quickly, his nervous excitement causing him to rush his bow. "I thought you ought to know that Tibbott Bourke has now been captured. Please allow me to assure you that he is held securely. He cannot escape."

"The boy has been imprisoned? He is no longer free.

Very good. And does he confess to his treason?"

"He has spoken very little, Your Majesty. He certainly does not confess anything, but merely asks to see his chieftain."

"And who is this chieftain? Where is he now?"

"The chieftain, Your Majesty, is the boy's mother. She—"

"What?" Elizabeth blinked, wondering if she'd misheard.

Lord Bingham gulped: "Your Majesty?"

"You say the boy's chieftain is his mother? A female captain?"

"That—that is correct," he stuttered.

"How extraordinary. And do we know where this *female* chieftain is now, Lord Bingham?"

"She remains on the west coast of Ireland, on Clare Island."

"And her name?"

"Gráinne O'Malley, Your Majesty." His palms were beginning to sweat as he rubbed them together. Elizabeth stood and moved closer to him now, and he could smell the natural scent that lingered on her pale skin. He couldn't help but notice the eager look that had flared in her eyes.

"Seize her and bring her to me then."

"You—you wish to see Gráinne O'Malley?"

"That is what I said, was it not?"

"Yes, yes. Certainly, Your Majesty. Right away."

"You may go now."

Elizabeth turned her back and paced to her chair by the window. Lord Bingham bowed behind her and scampered out of the room, having accepted his mission. He had a duty to do and he could not let Her Majesty down. He must do whatever was required of him to find this female captain and bring her to the Queen.

Gráinne O'Malley must be captured.

10

Grace's heart had raced when she heard the news, her head weightless and dizzy. She turned pale as Donal grabbed onto her to steady her on her feet. If only in that moment, she was overcome with emotions that were not her own. In those minutes following the news of his capture, she knew also that she had known Tibbott, and that she had loved him as her own.

They sat around the wooden table in the kitchen that Donal had led them to. Grace tried to remain calm as she studied the room. It became apparent that she was currently in the O'Malley household—this was *Gráinne's* kitchen—and part of her felt as though this were the most natural place in the world for her to be, a sense of belonging, a familiarity, and it provided her with a peculiar comfort that she hadn't expected.

There was certainly no doubt in the minds of Donal or Cathleen that she belonged there. As far as they were concerned, she was Gráinne O'Malley. They didn't seem concerned in the slightest by the difference in her accent or her lack of understanding of pretty much everything they said to her. They had no knowledge of Grace Byrne, and that didn't seem to matter to anybody. Right now, Grace had to put her own identity aside and concentrate on helping them.

"When did this happen?" she asked.

"Yesterday. Word only reached us this hour."

"Who was it?"

"Lord Bingham's men: I can't be certain Bingham was there himself, but it would not surprise me if he were. His thirst for blood has grown barbaric over the years. I should wonder whether or not he has any control over his own desires anymore." Donal's knee bounced up and down as he pumped his foot in agitation.

"Oh, this is just terrible!" Cathleen interrupted, wailing.

As much as Grace could have done without the girl's dramatic outburst, she knew she was right. There had only been one short paragraph about Tibbott in the article she'd read, but for reasons she couldn't explain she'd found herself drawn to it, and ended up reading it several times. She had learned about this situation, and she knew just how serious it was.

"What should we do?" she asked Donal.

"I was hoping you would have an idea."

"Me?"

"Gráinne, I trust you with this. We all trust you. We know you'll do the right thing. If it were down to me, I would hunt Bingham down and charge straight at him with the sharpest sword I could find, but even I do not believe that that it would be the right thing to do. Not when Tibbott's life is at risk."

"My son..." Grace spoke the words in a whisper with her head bowed toward the table, trying to absorb the situation, and overcome with the emotions that once had belonged to Gráinne. She had carried the boy, endured the pains of childbirth, and spent the subsequent years raising him and watching him grow. How awful it must be, as Grace was now discovering, to hear that one's child has been captured and is locked up somewhere far away.

"Oh, Miss Gráinne!" Cathleen rushed to Grace's side and knelt on the floor beside her. She clutched Grace's left arm and began to sob. 'We must save him; he's too young to die!'

Donal shot her a glance which she instantly understood as a sign to be quiet. She sniffed, wiping the back of her hand over her eyes to dry her tears. "I'm sure that Tibbott will come to no harm; we just need to find a way to bring him back to us. I have every faith that Gráinne will think of something, but in the meantime perhaps we should all use our heads a bit more to try to come up with a plan. And Cathleen, I would prefer it if you didn't spread this around the island. The fewer people who know about Tibbott's capture the better. At least until we can work out what we're going to do, then we can alert the necessary people. Honestly, I can't believe he would do such a thing. He wasn't prepared for it. He never would have succeeded in that state."

"Why did he do it?" Grace asked, already knowing the answer in her heart.

"He is just as fed up as we are, Gráinne. I do not blame him for wanting to fight against Bingham. We are losing more and more land each day, and what little supplies we have left for food are not exactly in the best of condition. Tibbott is fighting for what is rightfully ours, as we all are. He just didn't manage to time it right. It wasn't organised properly. We will defeat the English, Gráinne, I promise..."

Grace was starting to feel more like Gráinne O'Malley than Grace Byrne, but there was still a large part of her that felt out a character. There were times when she felt as if she were possessed by Gráinne's spirit, as if her own had been taken over, but she had to remind herself that she wasn't really Gráinne, was she? And Tibbott wasn't really her son. And she lived in England now. How would Donal react if he found that out? She wanted to confess everything, to stand up and shout that she wasn't really who they thought she was, but even if she decided that doing so would be a good idea, they would likely not believe her. They'd say she was delirious. She wasn't sure what the protocol was for signs of weak mental health in the sixteenth century, but she was certain that appearing to be mad would not do anybody good. As long as she was wearing Gráinne's boots, she had to be Gráinne.

Deciding to remain quiet about her true identity, she went along with the situation. She had to confess to herself that it wasn't too difficult to do. She had a great deal of compassion for Tibbott, something which she could not describe. Not only did she feel that it was her duty to rescue Gráinne's son, but it was something she knew she ached for too.

"How long do you think we have?" she finally asked.

"I'm afraid there's no way of knowing. Although we cannot be sure what Bingham will do to him now that he's locked up, we cannot take any risks. We must act as quickly as possible, that much is certain."

"Yes, of course. I'll think of something. It's not going to be easy though.'

"Nothing is ever easy with that brute Bingham."

"Poor, poor Tibbott," Cathleen added.

"He just never seems to stop. You know how difficult things are now, and I'm certain that all of it is Bingham's fault. We are losing more and more each day. If it continues much longer, I dare say we won't have anything left. There'll be no cattle or land to call our own."

"Whatever are we going to do?" Cathleen wailed once more.

"The harsh weather is a threat to our crops, which are already in a diminished state. Our land isn't just rapidly declining because of that thief Bingham—what little we do have left is also deteriorating in quality. Even if he left us what remains, we would still struggle to produce enough."

Grace could tell that times were difficult for them, but she hadn't quite realised the extent of the situation until now. Their misfortunes made her reconsider the effects of the financial problems everybody was facing back home in her own century, and just how insignificant it was for many in comparison.

"He will be okay, Gráinne, won't he?" Cathleen had finally calmed down but still clung loosely to Grace's arm.

Grace turned to look at her: "Of course he will be, Cathleen. Don't worry."

How she prayed that she was right.

"Good evening to you, Chieftain." The man nodded at Grace. He and another were humping a bundle of straw down the hill when she noticed them. She smiled at them, not paying too much attention to the fact that she had no idea why they were calling her that, but instead thought to herself that it was quite a peculiar time to be working outside in the darkness.

The wind picked up as Grace crossed over the hill. She had left Donal and Cathleen together in the kitchen. Donal suggested she might be able to think more clearly if she went up to her castle—which Grace assumed was Donal's code for encouraging her to escape from Cathleen's hysterics—and Grace's curiosity had overruled the situation. Ordinarily she would not have taken too kindly to being left alone in an old castle in the middle of nowhere on her own at night, but she had been mesmerised by it when she first saw it, and had been longing to take a closer look.

She pulled a woollen shawl tighter around her neck as she continued over the grass. Cathleen had fetched the garment for her before she left, insisting that she wear it so that she didn't catch her death outside. Grace was thankful for the gesture as the evening had turned bitter cold. The material may have been scratchy against her neck, but at least it prevented the wind from reaching her skin.

The houses behind her grew smaller in the distance as she approached the castle. She stopped a few metres outside of it so that she could study its structure. It wasn't what she would have pictured when she considered a castle. There was no drawbridge. It had no moat. There was no sign of any flag flying from the top of it. It was considerably smaller than Grace would have imagined, too.

In the darkness the castle's grey stone walls looked a lot more intimidating than they did when Grace had caught a glimpse of them in daylight. She didn't wish to look directly up at the windows out of the fear that she'd end up seeing a face staring back at her.

The entrance to the castle was facing her now. A little way in the distance she could see the ship. The sea stretched out before her, the castle standing a few metres away from the edge of the island. She could almost feel the sea clinging to her as the waves sprayed and splashed, thrown about by the wind. She clutched onto her shawl and headed for the door.

The entrance was situated inside a small shelter as a grey stone corridor reached out from the main building. It was barely two metres tall and not so long, but it was enough to keep the wind away from Grace's face. She stood in the little corridor, sheltered, facing the door.

The door itself was made of a dark wood. Thin copper strips ran down its front to strengthen it. The handle itself was made from iron, the metal hoop rusting in age. Beneath it Grace noticed a small keyhole, not dissimilar from the one on the door at the top of the landing back in Hampstead.

It suddenly occurred to her that she didn't have a key for the castle. If the door was locked she wouldn't be able to get inside.

Grace placed one hand on the handle and wrapped her fingers round it. The metal was cold against her bare hand. Hoping that the door wasn't locked, she turned the handle counter-clockwise and pushed.

The heavy wood only budged an inch to begin with, taking much more effort than Grace had expected. She leaned her weight against it and forced it open just enough for her to squeeze her body through and into the castle.

It was much darker inside the castle than it was outside. A few candles were placed upon the walls, white pillars resting inside purpose-built stone pockets. They were already lit, just as the one on the ship had been. She blinked a few times, adjusting to the dim lighting.

Directly in front of her, against the castle's right wall, stood the bottom of a staircase, the steps embedded into the stone. She couldn't see what lay at the top of them as they spiralled out of sight. To her left was a small doorway, arched at the top. Leaving the stairs for the meantime, she crossed through the doorway and entered a long rectangular room. The floor was made of the same stone as the exterior of the castle; she was thankful at that moment for the protection Gráinne's boots provided her from the cold, coarse surface.

It shocked Grace to find that this room, aside from the several lit candles that were evenly spread out along the walls to allow her just enough light to see, was completely empty. She walked further into the room to where the arrow-slit window was on the back wall. It allowed a little trickle of the natural moonlight from outside to cast a faint silver glow onto a pile of jagged rocks that sat in the far corner. Grace bent down and picked one up.

She held the rock in her hand then gave it a gentle squeeze to confirm its physicality. "How can this be real?" she wondered aloud, her voice but a whisper. "How can I be here? I don't understand..."

She sighed, accepting that there was nobody there to respond to the desperation in her voice, and brushed away her frustration as she let the rock drop back onto the pile with the others. Straightening up, she walked back to the archway. The room resembled little more than a ruin. If it weren't for the candles, then she never would have guessed it was inhabited.

With nothing else to see on the ground floor she

started up the stairs. Although her pathway was guided by the soft glow of the candles, she took caution as she felt out each step with the toes of the boots. The steps seemed to be secured quite well, but she could not afford to make a wrong move. If she slipped and fell, there would be nobody here to help her.

She followed the winding staircase, occasionally pressing her hands against the walls to balance herself in the narrow space, until she reached the first stopping point. As with the lower level, a few candles lined the walls to provide her with a source of light. However, much to Grace's disappointment, this floor was little improvement on the previous.

The space was much larger, with two archways dividing the floor into two square rooms. The floor, Grace noticed, was wooden, though not polished or even. It was pale and worn, as if it had stood the test of four centuries. Grace had expected to find the castle in the condition it had been in during Gráinne's lifetime. There was no way for her to work out whether or not it had looked this way in the sixteenth century, or if this is what it would look like if she visited it in her own time. Either way, she wasn't particularly fond of it. There was a strong draft in the room coming from the two square windows, one situated in each section, and it was starting to make her wish that she was back outside.

Thinking she'd not find much on the third floor either, Grace climbed the rest of the stairs. At first glance, everything was as she had expected: the floor was made from rugged wood, and the walls were bare, with the exception of the occasional lit candle. This room was also apparently divided; not all was visible at once. From where she stood she could make out another archway at the end of a narrow corridor, but she was unable to see what lay beyond. She proceeded through the corridor, her enthusiasm for the exploration of the castle dampened by the bleakness of the previous two floors, expecting to be just as disappointed by this room as she had been by the rest. It was only as she approached the archway that she noticed the light glowing in the room beyond it.

The light emitted the same soft glow as the other candles, except it couldn't be coming from just one candle—it was far too bright. She stood still, unable to see directly into the other room. Had the entire castle been lit this brightly then she would not have given it a second thought, but it seemed peculiar that the rest of the building remained in near darkness except for this one room. Breathing deeply, she closed her eyes for a moment, giving herself a second or two to gather her thoughts. Whatever she might find in that room, she had to be ready for it.

Grace turned the corner and gasped as she stood under the stone archway: *Gráinne's bedroom?!*

Unlike the damp grey spaces she had previously witnessed, this room was a welcoming display of warmth and colour. Narrow and rectangular in shape, a window was situated almost directly opposite the archway, about eight feet away from where Grace stood. It was square and had nothing to protect it, just an open space in the wall. For some reason though, this room appeared much warmer than the others, and the breeze she had felt downstairs didn't seem to be as strong in this room. Grace didn't think that this would have had anything to do with the thin curtains that hung at either side of the window. The cream fabrics were the length of the window and no more, and peculiarly remained almost still, as if the entire room were at peace.

To the side of the window stood a desk of a fair size, made from a rich mahogany. Three deep drawers ran down one side, each with a golden sphere for a handle. A matching chair stood in front of the desk, with both its back and legs hand-crafted into curves. Grace was sure they weren't products of Ireland. *Trade*, she thought to herself. *Or piracy...*

A bed was situated to the left of the desk. It was made

from the same dark wood as the rest of the furniture, with matching golden spheres on the end of each of the four bedposts. A bed sheet was draped over it, a silk the colour of blood, finished with gold stitching. Two pillows sat plump at the top of the bed, dressed in a cloth to match the cover. Still rooted to the spot in the archway, Grace paid particular attention to the size of the bed; it was smaller than the double bed she had at home, but considerably larger than any single bed she'd seen, and higher off the ground too. She couldn't help but admire it.

The desk and the bed seemed to take up most of the room; it was little more than a box at the top of the castle. Grace moved forward so that she stood at the centre of the room, and realised that she could move little further. There was a small space behind the desk, and just enough room between the furniture to move in front of the window, but it allowed for no other movement.

Grace turned her back on the bedroom for a moment as she crossed to the window. With the curtains already open she could see the ocean. Just a few metres away the waves ebbed away from her, the moonlight reflecting a silver shimmer onto the water's surface. The wind had softened. Everything looked peaceful. In the distance, the ship stood strong, still and silent. Lost in the beauty of the ocean, Grace momentarily forgot why she had entered the castle in the first place.

'Tibbott!' She startled herself with her own sudden outburst. She threw a hand in front of her mouth, worried that somebody outside might hear her. She looked below. Nobody was there. She slumped onto the chair in frustration.

"They think I'm Gráinne O'Malley. *Grace* O'Malley," she said, reminding herself of the connection. "But I'm not!" What did she really know about Gráinne? Aside from the Irish blood, which Grace was certain was just a coincidence, there seemed to be little they had in common.

She groaned, placed her elbows on the desk in front of

her and rested her head in her hands. "Why am I here?" She worked her fingers through her hair and massaged her temples. She stifled a yawn as she tried to concentrate on coming up with a plan to rescue Tibbott, but her mind could think of nothing. She considered returning to the ship to go back home. But the door had closed behind her when she'd entered again, and there was no telling whether or not it would ever be open again.

Grace approached the window again. As she stuck her head out slightly the cool night air brushed against her pale cheeks. It was refreshing, but as soon as she had exposed her face to the outdoors, the wind began to increase. Grace drew her shawl tighter. As she took a step back from the window, as if on cue, the rain started to fall. It was heavy enough to be heard as it collided with the stone walls of the castle. The sea crashed unnervingly in the distance.

With nowhere else to go, she would have to sleep in the bed in the castle. Grace turned to face it, studied it. It looked comfortable enough, but there was something playing on her mind. This bed belonged to Gráinne O'Malley. No matter what Cathleen or Donal thought, she knew this wasn't her bed, and she wasn't sure she'd feel right sleeping in it.

Understanding that she had little choice, she took hold of a corner at the top of the bed cover and pulled it back a little to discover that the mattress was covered with a thin sheet. I wonder if it's one she slept on, Grace thought to herself. Could the furniture around her possibly be from Gráinne's time? She promised herself she'd do whatever she could to find out in the morning, but right now, she needed to sleep.

Just as she was about to lie down, she noticed that something was sticking out from underneath the pillow. She lifted it to reveal a cotton nightdress. Holding it in front of her with a hand on either sleeve, she inspected the material. There was little shape to the nightdress, rendering it little more than a long white sheet. The neck of the garment was high, and its sleeves were narrow at the cuffs. Grace observed its length as she pulled it toward her body. It draped down to the same length as her skirt, settling around her ankles. While Grace knew the garment would keep her warm, she wasn't sure how comfortable it would feel.

Assuming the nightdress had been provided for her, she began to pull Gráinne's boots off her feet. She wiggled her toes as she removed each boot, before standing the pair at the foot of the bed. She took off her shawl, before allowing her fingers to work at the lace on her bodice, pulling and untying until she was completely free. It was only when she'd slipped it off that she realised just how tight it had been.

The chemise followed the bodice, and she folded them both into a neat pile on the desk chair alongside the shawl. She slipped out of the skirt and stood at the centre of the room, wearing only an undergarment smock. The chill of the room started to encircle her bare legs even beneath the fabric. She reached for the nightdress and pulled it over her head to escape the draft. It took her a moment to adjust to the long neck as the itchy material scratched at her skin.

Glancing around, she made sure that everything appeared to be in order before she settled down for the night.

"I'm not sure I should feel this relaxed in a stranger's bedroom," she said, with a smile spreading across her face. But she had to admit that she was actually starting to enjoy this adventure. It was a refreshing change from her mundane life, and now that she was no longer terrified, she was able to look at everything in a new light. Her thoughts and actions were now driven by three things: natural curiosity, a desire to succeed, and a mother's love for her son. People were counting on *her* to save Tibbott, and she wasn't prepared to let anybody down, especially not

Gráinne.

Grace drew the curtains closed. The rain was still falling and the wind still licked at the curtains, but she hoped it would be enough to keep most of the chill from engulfing the room throughout the night.

She turned to face the candles on the desk. They still flickered. She cupped a hand behind the first one and blew. The flame went out with a puff. She moved to the second one and repeated the motion. It extinguished. Now the room was in total darkness.

Sliding her feet along the bare wood, she made her way toward the bed. She used her hands to guide her to the mattress as she sidled along near the back wall, manoeuvring through the narrow gap. When she reached the top of the bed, she shuffled herself under the covers and lay down on her side, pulling the cover up to her chin. It was much softer than she had expected it to be, the blanket warm and comforting. She placed her head on the pillow and closed her eyes.

As she slipped into sleep, she didn't consider the strange surroundings in which she lay. She didn't think about how far away she was from her home in England. She didn't need to acknowledge that she was in a different century to that which she was accustomed. It didn't matter what her name was. It didn't matter where she was from or how she had arrived here. If only for a moment, as she escaped into her dreams, she had completely forgotten all about Grace Byrne.

11

A young girl twirled across the deck of a ship, her dark auburn hair wild and free and tangled hopelessly by the sea breeze. She bounded over to the side of the vessel and gripped onto the rail, before tilting her body so that she could look down onto the water. She inhaled deeply, the fresh smell of the sea filling her nostrils. She had never felt more alive.

"Gráinne O'Malley!" said a voice from behind her, "how many times do I have to tell you?"

The child turned to see her father standing with his hands on his hips and a scowl upon his face. He wasn't really mad at his daughter. How could he be? Anybody with a passion for the sea as strong as hers, and at such an early age as well, must be sound of mind. But he knew he couldn't let her come with them. It was much too dangerous for her.

"But—"

"No buts, young lady. You know the rules!"

"Please let me come with you, just this once," she pleaded desperately. There was an unmistakable maturity to her young voice.

"You know I can't allow it, Gráinne. As I've explained to you before, I do not have a problem with taking you out for a quick sail when I return, but voyages like these are not suitable for—"

"A little girl, I know." She crossed her arms and bowed her head.

"And I *did* tell you that as soon as I returned from Belclare it was very important that we were ready to leave again immediately. I'm afraid I just don't have time to take you anywhere just now." His words were firm but soft as he gestured for his daughter to leave the ship.

"Captain, we are ready." A young man emerged beside him. He was fresh and, as yet, untarnished by the sea.

"Thank you, Michael," the captain replied. "I will be along in a minute."

He bent down to his daughter's height.

"What's so wrong with me being a girl?" she questioned.

"Gráinne, it's just that the sea is no place for—"

"What if I shave my head? Pretend to be a boy? Then would you let me come with you?"

"I would rather you did not do that, my child! Perhaps you will be able to come with us one day."

"When will you let me?" she sighed.

"Soon, I promise."

"How soon?"

She showed no sign of giving up. She already knew that the ship was her destiny.

The father sighed. How could he deny her anything? She was the apple of his eye. "How about if we discuss this when I return, and we shall see if we can come to an agreement?" The child's face lit up. She beamed at her father. He leaned forward and embraced her in a hug, his ritual before leaving the island. "Go on now, Gráinne. I'll see you when we return."

She skipped off the ship, her head swimming with fantasies about the adventures she would soon be having on board with her father.

And he watched as she moved out of sight, knowing she would not forget his promise, and knowing too that she was indeed born for the sea.

Grace bolted upright in a sweat. She was certain she had been falling. She steadied her breathing, regained her balance. The low sun bled through a gap in the curtains, forcing her to adjust to the brightness. Her head still full with scenes of young Gráinne. She may nearly have slipped through the cracks in history, but to Grace she was very much alive.

But something was different. Something had changed. When she was finally fully awake, she sprang out of bed, flung back the curtains, and raced out of the room.

How could this have happened? She was back in her own bedroom. She had fallen asleep in Gráinne's bed in the castle, in a completely different country four hundred years in the past, and yet somehow she had managed to wake up in her own bed.

She paused outside the door at the top of the stairs. It was shut. She grabbed onto the handle and turned it, twisting and pulling, but it refused to budge. She banged her hands against the door. "Cathleen! Donal! Can anybody hear me?"

It was no use.

She wondered if Harriet was home. Surely she would have been alarmed to hear Grace banging on the door. She didn't even know what time it was. She turned to find that Harriet's bedroom door was open, with Bella visibly curled up on the tidy bed. Harriet definitely wasn't in her room.

"Harriet?" she called down the stairs. She waited a few seconds. There was no response. She must have left for work already.

Grace rested her head on the door, both relieved that she didn't have to explain her outburst to anybody. It had become apparent to Grace that she had little control over when it was that she could and couldn't cross to the other side of the door. She tried to remember her thoughts and actions just prior to the last time it opened.

"Research?" she questioned, thinking back to all she'd discovered while reading through articles on the Internet. "I'd been reading about Tibbott, and then...yes! And then Tibbott's capture was revealed when I went back!" Her frustration had been replaced with excitement as she took a step away from the door. "Perhaps I simply need to read more about Gráinne before I'm allowed back through. That *has* to be it!" She grinned, satisfied with her revelation, and not bothered about the fact that she seemed to be talking to herself more than usual. Until she'd worked out a plan to save Tibbott, it didn't look like she would be allowed back through the portal.

Existing simultaneously in two different centuries seemed to make the week go by extremely slowly. How it was only Tuesday, Grace had no idea. She was struggling through exhaustion as her body fought against the strain of living two lives. She dragged herself out of the seat and headed over to the kettle.

"Would anybody care for coffee?" she asked. She looked up to realise only James was in the office. Everybody else had gone out to work on assignments.

"Thanks, Grace; that'd hit the spot," James called from his desk. "If one more person hangs up the phone on me..."

"Maybe it has something to do with the fact that you're phoning them up about a missing pigeon?"

"Birds matter too, you know!" Grace couldn't tell whether he was being sincere or sarcastic. "This was a prize-winning racing pigeon, and it's somehow just vanished! The guy who owns it said the bird would never just take off and not return, so I have to do a bit of investigation, you see? I've promised the owner and taken this on as my duty, because the police aren't going to bother with a missing pigeon."

"Right you are, James. Milk?"

"Yeah, please."

Grace stirred the coffees and walked over to James's desk. She handed him his mug, the cartoon faces of Wallace and Gromit staring back at her.

"Cheers. Quiet today, isn't it?"

"Tell me about it. I almost wish Mr Barrie was here to shout at someone."

James sat up in his chair. "You know, Grace," he paused, "do you think he'd give me time off next month? It's just that I want to take my girlfriend on holiday before Christmas but—"

"I wouldn't count on it, James. It's like asking Scrooge to let the workers away early on Christmas Eve. I'd put money on his answer being a firm *no*. But, by all means, if you're feeling brave enough, then ask him." She grinned before returning to her seat.

Only a handful of emails had been sent, and not a single letter had been delivered to the office. All the articles had already been posted on the social media sites and there wasn't much she could do until everybody else finished their work for the day. Perhaps she could just...

She opened a search engine to scavenge for something, anything that might help her regain entrance through the portal. She found numerous references, but before she began to read, she fished out a notebook from inside the drawer of her desk. It had been untouched for months, but at least now it would be put to good use. She unclipped the pen from the top of it to reveal little more than a few pages of doodled ladybirds and jack-in-the-boxes.

The used pages were discarded and tossed onto the desk. Grace etched Gráinne's name onto the top of the first page and positioned the notebook to her side, not prepared to stop until she found what it was she was looking for.

An hour or so later she discovered something that

made her gasp.

"Lord Bingham? Wasn't that the man who Donal said had captured Tibbott?" She scribbled down her findings. "And he worked for the *Queen*!"

Aside from a few weeks at secondary school that had been spent looking at the history of the British monarchy, Grace had to confess that she knew very little about Queen Elizabeth I. She tried to picture a portrait of her in her mind as she read further down the page. To Grace's surprise, she found out that Gráinne had actually ended up appealing directly to the Queen for her son to be set free.

She thought for a moment before it clicked.

"Is that what I need to do?" she asked herself. 'But I couldn't... Could I?"

The concept of coming face to face with a Queen of England was starting to make Grace's head spin. She had promised Donal she would do anything she could to rescue Tibbott. And she knew it was down to her to save him. But just as she was starting to feel comfortable with the situation, she was suddenly being thrown back into deep and murky waters.

"No, I couldn't. I'm not strong enough! And I wouldn't know how to get across the Irish Sea to England. There has to be another way. They've got the wrong person!"

Flustered, she closed the browser and tossed her notes onto the desk. The room had suddenly grown hot and stuffy. Grace felt choked. She needed to get outside, find some fresh air.

She headed for the main door. Only James was in the office, and he wouldn't miss her. She left the room, took the stairs, and left the building.

The chilly air had never felt so welcome before. She inhaled deeply as she tried to clear her mind. What was she to do? She couldn't turn her back. She didn't even know if she had any control over the situation, or if she were even *allowed* a say in what happened. But then she saw him, up ahead. A newspaper was folded under his arm, a takeaway coffee cup in his hand. He looked left, right, left again before crossing the road. He was heading down the street now, coming toward her. He glanced up. He noticed her. Then he smiled.

"Grace," he said, standing in front of her now. "Enjoying the sun, as it were?"

Of course the sky was overcast.

"Just clearing my head," she said. She checked to make sure she was smiling at him.

"Work getting to you again?" He wasn't laughing now, but speaking seriously to her, because he understood how she felt.

"'I just needed a little break. Listen—"
"Grace—"

They grinned at each other.

"You first."

"I was just going to say thank you for coming to the diner the other night. I know it probably wasn't how you had planned to spend your evening, and I just wanted you to know that I really did appreciate it."

"Andy, honestly, I had a really good time. I was actually going to ask if you maybe wanted to..." she could feel her face burning up, "...come over to my place this weekend so I could repay you with the meal we talked about. Nothing fancy or anything, just something—"

"That'd be lovely, Grace. Thank you." He smiled as his eyes met hers. Nobody said anything for a moment, until Andy's attention suddenly snapped back to the office. "I really need to go upstairs and type this interview. The boss will kill me if it's not done by the end of the day."

"Oh. Yes, of course."

"I'll see you in there."

Andy entered the building, leaving Grace leaning against the wall. She had to check to see that she was still rooted to the ground. He had said yes. She could hardly believe it, but he had said yes.

What was she going to cook? What was she supposed

to wear? Had they even agreed on a day? Her mind was flooded with questions about the impending date. No room in there for worrying about Tibbott—not now. His situation would be the same whenever she returned, whether in a day or a week by her present-day clock and calendar. After all, she had a life to live—here, now, in London, at Anchor, and maybe even with Andy... She returned to the building and headed up to the office, her smile as broad as she had ever known it to be. Cathleen and Donal would have to wait for Gráinne. Right now it was time for her to focus on something important: Grace's life.

12

"Can you not wait two minutes?"

Miaow.

"Okay. Have it your way!" Harriet tipped the dry biscuits into the bowl and placed it back on the plastic mat. Bella brushed against her legs and went for her breakfast. "I'm going back to my own now, if that's okay with you, your Fluffy Highness!"

Bella crunched her way through the dish of food.

"Morning..." Grace shuffled into the room as Harriet was sopping up the last of the egg yolk with a slice of bread.

"Morning! Ready for your big date tonight?"

Grace had not been able to think about anything else all week, but she still didn't feel prepared. "Not exactly." She pulled out a chair and sat opposite Harriet. "I still need to shop for the food. I don't know what to offer him to drink, or how many options I should have prepared. I don't know what to wear. And I can't seem to—"

"Grace, relax! You'll be fine. From what I've heard, he seems like a genuine guy, and if that is the case, then he's not going to care about what you wear. It's pretty obvious he likes you. Try not to worry. Stay calm and just enjoy yourself."

"I suppose you're right. I'm just so nervous that I'm going to mess everything up. What if I burn the food, or—"

"When was the last time you burned a meal?"

"Well, I can't remember, but—"

"You'll be fine. I promise! What are you cooking, anyway?"

"I hadn't quite worked that out yet. I'm not entirely sure what he likes. I was thinking lasagne, or maybe spaghetti—"

"Classic! I'd definitely go with spaghetti. And then you can each take one end of a strand and suck your way up until your lips meet in the middle..."

"Harriet!" Grace tried to sound stern but she couldn't prevent herself from giggling at the image.

"I'm only saying!" She stood up and put her plate into the sink. "Right, I better get off."

"Where are you off to?"

"Shopping," she sighed. Unlike Grace, Harriet loved clothes shopping. "The shops are going to be packed, but I don't have much choice. I completely forgot the Christmas party at work this evening. There's still a month until Christmas; I don't know why they couldn't put it off for a few weeks. I suppose it's cheaper for them to do it earlier, but it means I wasn't on the ball with making sure I had something to wear in time."

"Why don't you just wear something that's already in your wardrobe?"

Harriet laughed. "That would probably be the sensible thing to do, wouldn't it? No, I wouldn't feel right. Besides, I've had my eye on a particular dress for a while now and I'm hoping it's still available in my size. I'll need some new shoes too, of course. And maybe a new bag as well. Oh, this is going to take all day. And don't worry, I'm staying over at Daniel's tonight, so I won't be in your way."

They'd agreed that Andy would arrive at seven, which would give her plenty of time to get ready and prepare the food, but how was she supposed to fill an entire day when her mind was racing ahead to the evening? She had struggled all week to stay focused at work—it didn't help that Andy sat directly in her view—and now that their first real date was swiftly approaching she was able to think of nothing else.

Preparing for dates and entertaining dinner guests weren't exactly at the top of her list of expertise. "First, the shopping," she said, placing her laptop on the coffee table before heading up the stairs. In her bedroom she started picking through a pile of clothes she'd left on the chair. She pulled on a pair of stonewash jeans and slipped a grey angora jumper over her head. She'd had the jumper for several years now and the material had started to thin a little at the sleeves, but it would have to do. She wrapped her hair into a bun to keep it out of her face. Retrieving her duffel coat from the wardrobe, she slipped it on and fastened it before pulling on a pair of ankle boots she'd bought during the Christmas sales last year. She hadn't had a chance to wear them yet, but she decided today was as good a day as any to bring them out. She checked to make sure her umbrella was still in her bag. The weather was dry but she just knew that if she didn't take it with her the heavens would open and she'd be drenched before she'd even reached the shop.

As she moved to close her bag her hand nudged against the letter from Gráinne. She held it in front of her for a moment and studied the writing on the front of it. She still couldn't believe that it was her name that she was reading. She stuffed it back into her bag, refusing to give it another thought. She needed to clear her mind before she approached that situation, and it was not time to do that now. She knew she would find the right answer eventually.

She grabbed her mobile phone from the coffee table and sent a text message to Andy.

Still on for this evening? Grace x

It was only after she'd sent the message that she wondered whether or not the kiss was too much. The last thing she wanted was to scare Andy off when things might just be getting started. Her heart raced as she waited for him to reply.

She need not have been concerned though. As soon as she had locked the front door behind her, her phone alerted her that a new message had arrived. She reached for her phone and flipped up the screen.

Of course! Remind me of your address and I'll be there at seven. Andy x

"Thank goodness!"

Looking around, she was relieved to find that nobody had heard her talking to her phone screen. She replied accordingly before returning the phone to her pocket and heading down Haverstock Hill.

A few minutes later she reached a cluster of shops opposite the underground station in Belsize Park and headed into Budgens. There were several supermarkets nearby from which she could quite easily purchase her supplies, but she'd been drawn to this one ever since moving to the area. Perhaps it was the bright green sign above the entrance, or maybe it had something to do with the fact that the bustle of shoppers that so often flooded the larger chain stores hadn't infiltrated the friendlier atmosphere of Budgens. Whatever it was, she always seemed to have a successful trip, and she was counting on today being no different.

She started up the first aisle with a basket swinging from her arm. She was relieved to be doing something normal, a welcome respite from the thought of returning to Clare Island that so frequently seemed to occupy her mind nowadays. Eventually she was satisfied that she'd found everything she was going to need.

Grace made her purchase, exited the shop, and turned back toward Hampstead. She decided to kill some time with a stroll; she wouldn't be going too far, and the mince should be okay for a short time.

She'd often take a stroll to Primrose Hill, or up to Hampstead Heath, when she wanted time outdoors to think—some of her best decisions had come to her that way. But her feet seemed to have a mind of their own as they crossed over the road toward Church Row.

She found herself heading toward the churchyard of St-John-at-Hampstead. She approached the gate and entered the grounds. The church itself stood directly in front of her, with one of its large red doors left ajar after Morning Prayer. Rather than enter, she decided to occupy one of the wooden benches situated beneath a cluster of tall trees. The breeze carried the leaves down one by one as they floated toward the ground, landing in a bed of brown and orange. Some of the leaves were wet from the rain, creating a slippery surface near the edges of the graveyard, and Grace took care as she approached the bench so that she didn't fall.

She sat down safely and looked at the gravestones. Some dated back hundreds of years, plant life nearly covering them. As she became lost in her thoughts a woman sat beside her. Grace had not heard her approach and was startled when she spoke.

"Do you believe they can help you?"

A thick Irish accent came with her words. It was different than Grace's accent, and that of any of her family. The mysterious woman stared straight forward, her attention fixed somewhere in the churchyard. Her eyes were watery pools of green, glistening like emeralds.

Dressed in a long sea-green smock, her attire didn't seem to fit the current century. The upper part of the cotton fabric took the shape of a bodice; the edges were stitched with a gold-coloured thread, and the material was tied tightly down the front with thick string to draw in the dress around the woman's thin frame. A woollen shawl was draped over her shoulders, the sleeveless garment reaching down to her hands. Her fingertips clasped its edge to keep it in place, protecting her pale arms from the wind. Her auburn hair was tied back into a long plait, reaching down to her waist. Grace noted that its length was longer than her own. The tight hairstyle pulled slightly at the woman's forehead, accentuating the delicate features of her face. Her nose was thin and long as it pointed towards her lips. Her lips were narrow but rich in their pink colour. This same shade highlighted the apples above her gaunt cheekbones, adding a small amount of colour to her otherwise-ghostly white skin.

"I'm sorry?" Grace finally managed to reply. She had been so mesmerised by this woman's sudden and striking appearance that she'd almost forgotten to respond to her question.

"Do you believe it's possible for those who are no longer of this earth to help in life as it is lived today?"

"I don't know..." She had no idea how to respond to a question like that. Grace's confusion grew as the woman continued to talk. Her voice was soft and gentle, but her words were insistent and unexpected.

"Do you not believe that there are ways in which those who have returned to the world of spirit can guide those on earth? Their physical bodies may be rested in the ground, but their spiritual bodies—their original forms—are still here. They are constantly around, working where their assistance is required. Do you not believe that they are able to help you?"

"I've n-never..." Grace stuttered. It wasn't something she'd ever considered, and she certainly was not prepared for the question to be thrown her way today. Not wishing to anger or upset the woman, she forced herself to recall the religious teachings she'd received as a child.

"I am not speaking about religion," the woman continued, as if she had been reading Grace's mind. "The spirits guide those who require it, and those whose minds are willing and open, regardless of their faith. They do not operate within religious constraints. Perhaps you are aware of Guardian Angels, or maybe even Spirit Guides. The concept is the same, except these spirits have simply been ordinary people on earth, just as you are now. They have no special rank, and they have no requirement for one. They have their duties, and with those they are able and content. There is no restriction between centuries, no language barriers across time or place. You are never alone, Grace."

Grace wasn't given time to consider how this woman could possibly know her name, because at that moment her phone sounded loudly from inside her pocket. She flinched as she reached for it, then turned away from the woman to silence the sales call. But as Grace turned again to face her, the woman had disappeared. Where had she gone?

Though, had her phone not caused a distraction, Grace would have noticed as the woman had walked along the path and out through the trees that a pair of leather boots were visible beneath her dress, and she would have also realised that the boots that the woman wore were identical to the pair that she had first discovered on board the ship, the very pair she wore to guide her along Gráinne's journey.

13

"*S*paghetti prepared, oven preheated, apron on!" Grace talked herself through her mental check-list as she tied the ribbon behind her back. "I think that's everything," she confirmed to herself as she arranged walnuts on top of a sponge cake. As she slid the baking tray into the oven her phone sounded from across the table. She sighed as she recognised the caller instantly. "Hello, Mum."

"Grace, it's Mum." Her accent was much stronger than Grace's.

"How is everyone?"

"Everyone's fine, dear. Your Dad says hello."

"Hello to Dad," she said.

"Listen, did you receive the photograph I sent you on that e-thing this morning?"

Grace had lost count of how many times her Mum had phoned her asking how to send an email. She was learning, slowly, but Grace still wouldn't dream of letting her loose on her own laptop.

"I've not checked my emails today, Mum."

"Are you in the house now? You need to see this!"

"Well, I am at home but I'm kind of—"

"Turn on your computer and have a look!" Mrs Byrne interrupted. "Oh, you'll love it, Grace!"

With little other choice, Grace glanced at the oven to make sure it was okay before dashing through to the living room.

"Right, I'm booting it now," she responded as she opened the laptop. The machine whirred to life. "What is it you want me to see?"

"You'll find out when you open it. Have you got it yet?"

"It takes a minute to load. Right, here we are." She found the email and clicked it open. It was never a good sign to find an attachment from her Mum. She scrolled down and located the photograph at the bottom of the page. There was no challenge in identifying her Mum near the centre of the gathering, and around her stood faces Grace also recognised. There were a few people nearer the edges of the photo she'd never seen before, but it was quite obvious whose family this was. "Is this from the baby's baptism?"

"It's from the baby's baptism! Just look at him, Grace. Isn't he adorable?"

She looked at the small pink child in the arms of her Uncle Seamus, a fluffy mop of bright ginger hair already forming on his freckled infant head. "Yes, I suppose he is..."

"They have a name for him now, too."

"It's about time. What did they go with in the end?"

"They've decided to call him Malachy Michael Martin MacBride," Mrs Byrne squealed.

"Wow, that's quite a mouthful!"

"He's just the sweetest baby, Grace. I wish you could have been there."

Apart from returning each Christmas, Grace seldom went been back to Belfast since she'd moved to England.

"Your Great-Uncle Malachy O'Malley was flattered at the name choice, of course. He spent the entire day tickling the baby's—"

"Did you say O'Malley, Mum?" The question had come out with more force than she had intended, but she needed to make sure she'd heard right. She had no recollection of ever having heard of this relative.

"Yes, dear. You've never met him before, and I've only really met him once or twice myself before last weekend. I must say, he's quite a handsome man. He's fourth from the left in the photo," said Mrs Byrne.

Grace studied the image on the screen. "I didn't know we were related to the O'Malleys, Mum."

"Only by marriage. He married my Aunt Nora—that's your Granny MacBride's sister—just before you were born. They live on the other side of the city though, and as you know, we never really speak to Aunt Nora unless we have to. Every time we've had to deliver a present or take something to them Malachy has been away on business. He's nearly ninety now, though. I expect he'll be at home a lot more nowadays. Perhaps I should pay my Aunt Nora a visit and see if he—"

"Is he from Mayo?" If there was even the slightest chance that this Great-Uncle of hers was related to Gráinne O'Malley, then she was going to make sure she found out about it.

"No, of course he's not from Mayo. He was born and raised in Belfast. I remember one time we were all sitting at the dinner table when you were just a baby, and your Dad mentioned to Granny MacBride that he had to go to Galway for a few—"

"Mum, I don't mean to interrupt"—Grace knew she was about to start another one of her never-ending stories—"but I really need to go. I'm baking a cake and I need to take it out of the oven before it burns." Having almost forgotten about the cake, she rushed back to the kitchen with the phone still to her ear.

"How lovely that you still bake! What is it this time?"

"It's a walnut sponge cake, Mum," she said as she

struggled with the baking tray.

"I do love a good sponge cake. Are you having friends over for a sleepover?"

"Sure, Mum." It was easier than telling her the truth.

"Enjoy your cake, dear; I'll phone you later in the week."

"Bye, Mum. I love you."

"I love you too, dear."

Grace hung up and dropped the phone onto the kitchen counter. She had fallen uncomfortably behind schedule now and was going to have to work quickly to catch up if she wanted everything to be ready before Andy arrived. She'd just about finished when her phone rang again.

She looked at the caller ID, and considered ignoring it. But what good would it do? She knew Caroline would only keep ringing until Grace eventually answered, and she'd rather speak to her now than have to face her conversations when Andy was around.

'Hello?"

"Grace, darling, it's Caroline!"

"Hel—"

"I'm glad I caught you. I tried ringing a few minutes ago but you must have been on another call. Listen, I wanted to thank you for coming over last week. It really was great to see everybody and catch up again, wasn't it? It's been so long." Grace was sure that Caroline wasn't phoning just to thank her. "It was such a fun night. I don't think I've laughed that much in ages. My cheeks are still hurting. Anyway, I was wondering if you were busy on Friday?"

There it was.

"Well, I'll be at work—"

"I need you to meet me on your lunch break. I've been given a new project, something we're publishing about the monarchy, and I've been asked to visit Westminster Abbey as part of the first article. But the thing is, Grace, I'm really not all that interested in that sort of thing, and I know you're quite keen on all that historical stuff, so I thought you'd be able to come with me, point out a few things, and then we can have something to eat. What do you say?"

"Okay, I can help you," she said. "But only for an hour—the boss will kill me if he knows I've been gone any longer."

"Oh you're a star, Grace. Thank you. I knew you wouldn't let me down. Perhaps you could do a little research for me beforehand, maybe jot a few things onto a piece of paper for me that I can take back to the office and work with..."

Caroline continued talking for another twenty minutes; it was proving impossible to hang up on her, as every time she tried to say goodbye Caroline launched into another story. But when she began to gossip about somebody in her office who had just undergone some awful cosmetic procedure, Grace knew she was going to have to interrupt.

"Caroline, I really have to go. I have somebody coming over soon. But I'll meet you outside the Abbey on Friday, I promise."

She hung up the phone and sprinted up the stairs, flinging off her apron as she went.She was covered in flour, and Andy was due to arrive any minute. She had to find something suitable to wear, and fast.

"Wow!"Andy stood in the doorway, poised with a bottle in his hand. "You look wonderful!"

"Thanks!" It wasn't much, but Grace had managed to dig out a teal summer dress from the back of her wardrobe—something a bit more feminine than the outfits she usually wore, she thought, but still comfortable. She studied Andy's choice of outfit with admiration: he was wearing a white shirt—undoubtedly a new purchase—with grey suit trousers, his black waterproof left unzipped to reveal the lack of tie around his neck. The top button of his shirt had been left unfastened, and there was a hint of stubble on his chin. Although unusual for Andy, it was much less than the beard upon Donal's face. Grace noted to herself that she'd never seen Andy look this relaxed.

"This is for you, Miss Byrne," he managed, bowing playfully as he handed her the bottle of wine.

"Thank you, that's very kind of you. Come in; I won't be a moment." She had been in the middle of drying the dishes when the doorbell rang. "Make yourself at home and I'll get some glasses." She hoped he wasn't able to detect the nerves in her voice as she showed him to the living room.

"Interesting artwork," Andy called when he noticed the multi-coloured painting above the mantelpiece.

"The horse? That's my housemate's. She's very big on animals," Grace replied. "She's out this evening though. Hey, you don't mind cats, do you?" She pulled the cork on the bottle.

"No, not at all. Why?"

Right on cue Bella crawled around the door and emerged at the side of the sofa, rubbing her arched back against the furniture.

"Never mind," Andy called as he reached down to tickle Bella on the back.

Grace entered the living room with two glasses of white wine and handed one to Andy. "Cheers!"

She decided to play it safe and sit on the sofa opposite him, not wanting to seem too forward by invading his personal space. She was a little surprised when he edged closer to her. He sipped at the glass and glanced around the room.

"So..."

"I've baked a cake." Grace was sure she hadn't meant it to come out as forced as that. She was just trying to prevent an awkward silence.

"Oh, brilliant! What kind?"

"Walnut sponge. I hope that's okay."

"Certainly. I don't believe there's a cake out there that I

won't eat. I remember my mum took me to this beautiful little café when I was a boy as a treat for doing so well on my report card for once in a subject that wasn't sport—I never really took any interest in writing until secondary school. She bought me this Belgian chocolate cupcake, and I can still remember the delicious aroma as the waitress placed it on the table in front of me, the sweet smell completely enveloping me in this sort of cocoon of chocolate perfection. It had these little flakes on the top and it crumbled wonderfully whenever I took a bite. To this day, I can't say I've ever had a better cupcake."

"It must have been delicious for you to remember it so vividly.'"

"It was! Sadly, I don't think that café's there anymore. Quite a shame really."

"Did you go there often?"

"Not really. It was a place that we'd go to if Sarah or I had done particularly well at school or some other activity. We didn't really have a lot of money when we were growing up. Our parents had decided to take out a mortgage on a house in Kensington before they realised that Mum was already pregnant. Several years down the line they were juggling house payments and two kids on one wage. We still had fun though. I always remember it being a happy home. It wasn't until they both died a few years ago and we had to sell the house that I realised how much I was going to miss that place."

"I'm sorry to hear that." Grace was surprised by how open Andy was being with her.

"It's okay. I suppose it's something you get used to, isn't it? You grew up in Belfast didn't you?"

"I did, yes."

"I've been to Dublin, but never as far as Northern Ireland. What's it like?"

"Well, I can't say it was the easiest of upbringings— always on guard, always on the lookout. But it's a beautiful place, so many hidden treasures if you get away from the centre."

"I'm sure I'd love to visit one day," Andy said with a hint of suggestion.

"You really should. I must admit that I often miss it."

"I'm ashamed to have to ask, because all this sort of stuff really does confuse me, but do you consider yourself to be British or Irish?"

Grace remained silent for a moment.

"Oh, I'm sorry. That wasn't the right thing to ask was it? I didn't mean to—"

"No, it's fine. Honestly. It's just something I have to think about as I'm not really too sure myself. There's a lot of division, you know? I'm never quite sure which nationality I consider myself to be."

"I understand. So you moved here to study then?" Andy asked, tactfully redirecting the subject.

The question made Grace realise that, in all the years they'd worked together, they'd never really sat down to have a proper conversation. Until recently they'd engaged in little more than office banter. While she wouldn't deny that she'd enjoyed that side of the relationship, she was glad that things seemed to at last be taking a new direction.

"I think I just fancied a change of scenery. I'd always wanted to visit London anyway, so it seemed like the perfect situation."

"And you have no regrets?" He drained his glass.

"None at all: I mean, yes, I wish I were enjoying my job more; and no, this wasn't where I thought I'd be at this stage in my life, but I have a lot to be thankful for, and I need to remind myself of that more often."

For a moment neither spoke. Grace was certain that this harmony could last forever. That was, until the timer sounded from the kitchen.

"Will you excuse me for a moment? I need to see to the food." She stood to leave the room.

"Sure thing," he called after her as he placed his empty glass on the coffee table. To occupy himself while he waited he turned his attention to a small pile of books at the foot of the table. He picked up the one on top to discover that it was a collection of poetry. "I didn't know you liked poetry, Grace."

"How can you be so sure it's mine?" she teased.

"Because it has your name written on the first page..."

"I'm not actually all that interested, to be honest," she said. "I thought I'd give it a go and bought a couple of books from a charity shop, but I never really took to it." She drained the pasta. "I was sorting through some old books to donate and thought those could go back."

Andy didn't respond, but instead he read the list of names out loud as he scanned the contents page. "Wordsworth. Coleridge. Blake. Byron—hey, I went to the same school as him," he confirmed to himself.

"Same school as whom?" Grace asked from the kitchen.

"Lord Byron," Andy called back. "I went on a scholarship." As he returned the book he noticed a bundle of papers that lay scattered near the books, and he couldn't resist the temptation to have a quick peek to see what mysteries they might contain. He picked up the top sheet and began to read, unaware that Grace was almost finished preparing the meal in the kitchen.

He was still holding up a sheet of paper when she returned to the living room.

"Dinner is served—" She stopped in her tracks.

"Oh, so sorry; I was just glancing over these while I was waiting for you. I hope you don't mind. I didn't know you were interested in pirates. Are the notes for anything special?"

What could she say to him? She could hardly tell him the truth. He'd think she had gone insane. Before Grace could respond though, there was a knock at the front door.

"Sorry, do you mind if I get that?" Grace dashed out of the room to see who it was, relieved for the opportunity to consider her response to Andy's question.

"Sorry about that. I had to sign for a parcel for Harriet. More online shopping, I assume," she announced when she returned.

"No worries," Andy replied as they made their way to the kitchen.

The subject of Grace's research didn't enter the conversation again, at least not immediately. Once they were seated at the table, the taste of the wine soon became the hottest topic of conversation. Grace served another glass, and then another, as both rapidly drained their drinks.

However, the inevitable was soon to happen, and Grace couldn't avoid it.

"So you never did tell me what those notes were for..." Andy revisited the topic as Grace was busy twirling a strand of spaghetti around her fork.

"I'm—I'm writing an article," Grace blurted out.

She had no idea where that had come from. She had panicked; it was the first thing that had popped into her head. And yet, somehow, it made perfect sense. Her mind now started whizzing with ideas.

"I think I'd like to read that when you're done, if you would let me of course. What I managed to read of your notes sounded interesting. And I take it this article will be shown to Mr Barrie?"

"I—yes, I suppose it will..." She could have squealed from her newfound excitement. She didn't know why she hadn't thought of it before. "Yes, I'm writing an article for Mr Barrie so that he'll see that I have greater potential and will hopefully offer me more responsibilities."

"Good for you! I'm glad you've finally thought of something. I was starting to worry that I'd have to force you to look for another job. The last thing I want is for you to leave Anchor, Grace, but I do hate seeing you unhappy."

Grace's mouth lowered from an excited grin into a

warm smile as she gazed at Andy, who stared silently across the table at her. She blushed, not accustomed to the attention, and lowered her head as she concentrated on working another strand of spaghetti.

Andy chuckled softly before continuing: "So tell me, what's this article all about? Your notes are about a female pirate, aren't they?" he asked.

'They are, yes. Her name is Gráinne O'Malley, or Grace—"

"That's your name," Andy pointed out the obvious.

"Yes, it is!But she's from the west coast of Ireland, and from the sixteenth century."

"Sounds fascinating... A female pirate is certainly not something I would have expected, especially not back then."

"Perhaps that's why she was so notorious," Grace responded, her eyes widening with the opportunity to talk about something she'd kept secret for longer than she cared to consider. "I think even today the idea of a powerful female is something with which society struggles, and such personalities were almost unheard of in her time."

"I can only imagine..."

"The islanders *are* feeling the strain of being under English rule," she remarked, not wholly conscious of her chosen tense, and forgetting that her so-called present circumstances in Ireland were otherwise in the past. "Their land is suffering in both size and quality, and both finances and food are of equal shortage."

"You sound as if you've been there," Andy laughed, not realising the importance behind Grace's words, but finding the passion in her expressions to be admirable. "English rule? Who was in charge at the time?"

"Queen Elizabeth."

"Ah, yes, good old Lizzie! She was quite a strong woman, wasn't she? What was it she'd said? 'I know I have the body of a weak and feeble woman, but I have the heart and stomach of a king!'" said Andy in his best female voice before wolfing down another forkful of spaghetti.

"Actually," continued Grace, "you wouldn't believe this, but Gráinne actually met the Queen. Her son was captured by one of Her Majesty's men. Gráinne had to go to England to fight for his release."

"Goodness! And how did that go?"

"I...I don't know," was her honest answer. "Do you expect she was frightened?"

"I can't imagine anybody would ever feel prepared to be standing in front of Elizabeth I, not even this notorious Grace O'Malley! One wrong move and you could have had your head chopped off before you knew what was happening. I dread to think how many executions were carried out..." He scooped up the last of the sauce. "I mean, can you imagine walking out into the street to find somebody's head being axed off right in front of you? I'm so glad public executions don't happen here anymore. I'm sure that we'd all be traumatised from it."

Grace caught her breath. She had been so worried about finding a way to save Tibbott that she hadn't even considered the dangers of visiting England in the sixteenth century, and she had no idea how her own timeline would be altered if she were to be captured just as Tibbott had been.

"I'm telling you, Grace, this is your chance to do the right thing!"

"The right thing, yes..." she murmured, her thoughts drifting.

"It's about time somebody stood up to Mr Barrie. I think your approach is just the wake-up call he'll need. You're a real warrior woman, taking on that man. He shouldn't be taking advantage of his staff. It's not fair that he gets away with treating us like we're dirt. It's not as if he'd be able to operate the business without us either!"

Grace stared as Andy chewed his food, smiling at her as he remained oblivious of the fears that were now invading her mind. She returned the smile weakly, but her attention was distant. She knew the pressure upon her to speak with Elizabeth I—and she knew she'd have to act on it soon—but fear held her back. As Andy raised his glass to toast the prospects of Grace's article, she started to consider the possibility that she might not actually make it back alive.

14

Caroline beamed at Grace as she approached the gates of Westminster Abbey.

"Grace, darling! I'm so glad you could make it." She leaned in to air-kiss her cheeks before draining the last of her takeaway coffee. "Ever had one of these toffee nut things?" she asked, gesturing to the festive polystyrene cup. "To die for!" She tossed the empty cup into a nearby bin and straightened herself up: "Right then, are we ready?"

"Sure. But I've got to be back at the office within the hour or my boss will go insane."

This wasn't entirely true: Mr Barrie had announced that he was going to an important business meeting and wouldn't be back all day. By the look of the golf clubs he had tried to sneak out of his office without anybody noticing, Grace was sure she'd be fine if she stayed a little longer, but she didn't exactly wish to spend any more time with Caroline that she had to. She was an old friend, but she could be quite a handful, too.

"Seriously, Grace, you need to get yourself out of that place. You're kept on such a tight lead. It can't be fun, surely! You really should look for something else."

"I know," Grace muttered as they approached the visitors' entrance. She wasn't in the mood to explain everything to her. Instead, she admired the grand Gothic architecture as it towered above them, a dark cloud floating in the sky casting alluring shadows over its features. "It's really quite beautiful, isn't it?"

"What? Oh yeah, sure," Caroline replied as she fished into her bag for her change purse. "I can't believe they charge us to get in here."

"I know what you mean. It doesn't seem right to have to pay to enter a place of worship. I suppose it goes toward the upkeep though."

"You think? Honestly, I don't know what all the fuss is about, but I thought I should make the effort for Archie."

"Archie?"

"That's *my* boss. He's really sweet. And very cute!"

Caroline paid for her entry and Grace walked up behind her, relieved to find that it wasn't as expensive as she'd anticipated. Maybe this visit would encourage her to start seeing more of the tourist attractions in London. There had been time for her to seek out a few things during her university days, but when she started at Anchor she found she simply didn't have the strength to go gallivanting around London; all she wanted to do on her days off was curl up on the sofa in front of the television or lose herself in a good novel. She had to confess that she had been looking forward to getting out in the open today to explore the Abbey, just as she had promised herself she would do for months but had never bothered.

"What language would you like?" asked a man handing out guide leaflets.

"English please."

He gave them both a leaflet, offered them the digital guide that was included in their ticket price, and moved on to greet the next visitors.

"We definitely don't need to bother with the digital guide things,' said Caroline as she opened the floor plan in her leaflet. 'We can head straight to wherever it is that the kings and queens are buried and then we can leave. We won't waste any time, don't worry."

"Right, okay." Apparently, Grace wasn't going to see as much as she had hoped.

"Did you manage to bring the notes I'd asked you for, by the way?"

"I did, yes." She handed her an envelope containing several sheets of information about the history of the building and those laid to rest inside it. Some of the facts she'd already known but some she'd had to research. It had kept her mind occupied throughout the week, which she'd been quite thankful for. After the fears Andy had put in her about the dangers of Elizabethan England, she wasn't sure she'd be able to go through that door ever again.

They'd had a lovely evening though, despite her concerns. It must have been after ten o'clock by the time he announced he had to head off. They'd spent most of the time after the meal drinking and talking, and, at one point, playing with a bit of string to tease Bella. It hadn't been awkward in the office that week either, but then Grace questioned whether or not there was actually any ground for it to be uncomfortable. She still wasn't sure whether or not it was a proper date, or if Andy had just agreed to the evening so she could repay him for the time they'd spent together at the diner. Perhaps she should just come right out with it and ask him.

But since the conversation they'd had that night everything had started to feel like a dream. Perhaps it was because she was going out of her way to ignore the past, but she hardly noticed the door now anyway, and she wasn't cut out for this. She *wasn't* Gráinne O'Malley. As long as she kept convincing herself of that, then she was certain it would just go away and she'd never have to deal with it again. It was time for her to take a step back.

"I believe she's in here," Caroline said as she jabbed at the map, pointing to a space marked *Henry VII's Lady*

Chapel.

"Where who is?"

"Queen Elizabeth I."

"That's who you're doing your project on?"

"I'm supposed to be looking at all the Tudor line and their relationship to contemporary London, but I thought she'd be a good place to start."

It must be a coincidence, Grace thought. They made their way around the building, manoeuvring around all the other tourists as they followed the marked route. They stopped at a monument rising from the floor. It was taller than either of them had expected, with bars all around it.

"It's quite large, isn't it?" remarked Caroline.

In the centre of it lay a marble carving of the Queen. The entire sculpture was all one colour, with the exception of her crown, which was incredibly detailed and well-crafted. She was well-protected, barricaded from interfering hands. Grace looked into the marble face, studying her features.

"It's quite creepy if you ask me," said Caroline, interrupting Grace's thoughts as she examined the face in front of her. "What was it she'd said? I have a king's body or something?"

Grace wasn't really listening. She was trying to comprehend the situation, fighting with herself to work out whether or not she could dismiss this coincidence without ignoring the obvious sign that lay right in front of her.

For weeks Grace had tried to force any thoughts of Queen Elizabeth I out of her mind. She had finally made the decision that she wanted nothing more to do with the situation and had determined to ignore the portal back to Clare Island.

And yet, she now found herself standing at the tomb of Elizabeth I. Her body wasn't in the sixteenth century anymore. She was right there, in Grace's own time. Even when carved on her own monument she still possessed a strong sense of power, but Grace couldn't help reminding herself of the fact that she no longer existed as a living person. Just like everybody else, she had faced her end. Nobody was immortal. As Grace looked upon the Queen's solid face, she realised what it was she was meant to see. She couldn't hide from it any longer. She knew what it was that she had to do. It was time for her to stop running.

She needed to speak with Queen Elizabeth I.

15

*T*he curtains flapped gently in the breeze as Grace curled the final letters of her signature. She'd never written with a quill and ink before. This was evident by the first few sentences of the letter, which were misshapen and frequently smudged. She'd wanted to start over, but there was precious few sheets of parchment in the drawer and she wasn't sure whether or not she'd be able to source any more. By the end, however, she'd managed to find a comfortable way to hold the quill, and had become used to dipping the tip into the ink just far enough so that the right amount could be distributed onto the sheet without running everywhere.

She'd spent the entire evening after visiting Westminster Abbey trying to work out what she was supposed to do. She rearranged all her notes, and then continued to rearrange them until she was certain she understood the situation. Once she felt certain enough that she'd approached it from all sides, she could do nothing but climb the stairs with her fingers crossed.

When she found that the door was finally ajar for the first time in days, she sighed with relief. It was the sign she had been hoping for that confirmed to her that she was doing the right thing. Crossing the threshold into Ireland, she knew that this was it. There was no going back now. She knew that she had to forget about her own existence for the time being and concentrate on the matter at hand. She belonged to the sixteenth century now, and all the inner strength she managed to conjure told her that she wasn't to return until Tibbott had been brought home. Now, all that was left to do was hope that everything went according to plan. There was no back-up option if she failed.

Back inside the castle, she stared out the bedroom window, trying to understand exactly what was required of her. She sat back, the material of her skirt catching in the drawer of the desk and nudging it open. Out of curiosity she teased it all the way to discover that it contained the instruments for letter-writing. She knew then what she must do.

She was faced with a peculiar sensation of delight when she sat down to write. She never could have imagined she'd be writing a letter to Queen Elizabeth I. Once she had confirmed to herself that she had to arrange an appointment with Her Majesty, sending this letter seemed like the only thing to do.

Unfortunately, she wasn't sure *how* to do it at first. Although she was feeling a lot more comfortable performing as Gráinne—*was* she still performing?—her way of speaking was still in tune with the twenty-first century. It would have been impossible for her to write as they had then. She glanced over the words in front of her, and then began to read them aloud.

'*I, Gráinne O'Malley, Chieftain of Clan O'Malley,*' she realised how easy the name had been for her to write, free of any self-doubt, '*wish to request an audience with Her Majesty Queen Elizabeth.* Or should that have been *Her Majesty the Queen*? Oh help!'

She read the rest of the letter to herself. She hoped that

what she'd written wouldn't be too disastrous. The last thing she needed right now was to anger the Queen of England as she thought back to what Andy had said about the public beheadings.

What an awful way to go! she shuddered to herself as she folded the letter. Whatever she had written was going to have to do. Besides, there was little parchment left, and even less time in which to write something else. She was just going to have to hope for the best.

"Why don't they just have normal envelopes?" she grumbled as she fiddled with the edges, trying to fashion it into something suitable. Once she had succeeded in creating a passable envelope, having almost resorted to origami, she turned her attention to the sealing wax. She'd positioned the solid stick of red wax at the top of the table next to the stamp when she'd sat down to write, admiring the beauty of the red and gold colours. Somehow, she expected using it would be much trickier to master than it would have appeared.

The only way she could think to do this was to reach for one of the candles in the room and hold it close to the stick of wax. To Grace's surprise—for not for a moment did she think her plan would actually work—the wax started to melt, obediently, and dripped right on top of the fold in the envelope to create a little crimson puddle. Not risking it drying too quickly, she returned the candle to its stand, and drove the stamp down onto the liquid wax. When she moved it away, she found that the stamp left a little crest in the wax. Inside the shape appeared to be some sort of horned animal, a bull perhaps, but it was hard to tell because the image was so small. Beneath the crest Grace could just make out a name: Ó Máille.

It suddenly occurred to her that she'd seen this image before when researching Gráinne's ancestry.

It's the O'Malley family crest!

Of course, it made perfect sense to her now—what else had she expected to find on the stamp upon the writing desk inside Gráinne O'Malley's castle?

When the wax had dried, Grace headed down the stairs. She was thankful that the candles were still burning; although the afternoon sky had yet to darken, the enclosed space allowed little light to be shed on the staircase. She left the castle, closed the door behind her, and crossed over the grass. She held onto the letter tightly, hugging it to her chest. It only took her a few minutes to reach the houses, but in that time her heart had begun to race. She had no idea what the others would think of her plan.

"Miss Gráinne!" Cathleen, who had been standing in front of the window of her family home, noticed Grace approaching and bounded through the door.

"Good afternoon, Cathleen. How are you?"

"I am quite well, thank you. Please come inside, Miss Gráinne. I am just setting the table as we are about to sup."

She led Grace through the doorway and into the kitchen. The room was smaller than the kitchen of the O'Malley household, but it was comfortable nonetheless. Although quite basic, and with little to offer in the way of decoration, Grace couldn't help feeling its warmth and welcome the moment she walked through the door, and the aroma that filled the air smelled so fragrant that she could barely stop her mouth from salivating. Cathleen steered her to an empty seat next to Donal, who had been there for half an hour conversing with Cathleen's family.

"I'm afraid it's not much today. The crops haven't been doing very well, have they Mr O'Flynn?"

"Unfortunately, there's too much truth in that statement, young Donal." Padraig O'Flynn was a short man with a round face, his cheeks tinted pink from constant labouring in the salty winds. But despite the hours of grafting that each day brought him, he always seemed to maintain his cheery disposition. "Good afternoon, Gráinne," he smiled to the new arrival.

"Good afternoon," she responded, not really sure who

it was she was talking to.

"Here you are, Daddy." Cathleen presented a plate of salmon and vegetables to Mr O'Flynn before placing one in front of Donal. Grace's plate followed, before Cathleen herself joined them at the table.

Grace waited for Mr O'Flynn to begin eating before she started herself. She decided to try the fish first as she couldn't quite discern what the vegetable portion was meant to be. With her stomach rumbling, she was delighted to find that it was exactly to her liking—better, in fact. She'd never eaten salmon as fresh as this before.

"Gráinne, there must be something we can do," Donal said as she was about to brave a vegetable.

"Well," she said, "I've thought about this carefully, and I've come to the conclusion that the only thing to do is speak directly to the Queen."

Nobody knew how to respond. Of course they were used to Gráinne's notorious behaviour—Grace was aware of that—but nobody had expected her to suggest something as outrageous as actually talking face to face with Queen Elizabeth.

"Gráinne, I don't think—"

"Donal, it does not seem that we have any other option." She could tell by the panic in Donal's eyes that this wasn't what he had wanted to hear. "I've written this," she said as she lifted the letter from her lap, "requesting an audience with Her Majesty. We need to send this to the mainland to have somebody take it over to England. Once that's done we can sail to London and free Tibbott." The plan sounded so much more straightforward when she said it out loud. But something told her it was going to be anything but easy.

"Gráinne, do you really think that's a good idea?" Donal didn't want to disagree with his sister, but he couldn't envision this plan working.

"Donal is right, Miss Gráinne!" Cathleen wailed. "It's much too dangerous. You know what they think of us over there, and how frightful it would be if you were to run into that wretched Lord Bingham!" A single tear trickled down her face as she thought about the trouble her beloved Miss Gráinne might face if she were to sail to England.

There was a grumble from across the table. They all turned to look at Mr O'Flynn, who was finishing his last mouthful of fish. He chewed and swallowed before speaking.

"I think we need to listen to what Gráinne is saying. Perhaps seeking out the attention of the Queen directly *is* the way forward." It was difficult to tell whether Mr O'Flynn actually believed in Gráinne's plan, or if he was just admitting that it was the only option they seemed to have that would allow them to at least attempt to bring Tibbott home.

One thing was certain though: he was right.

"But Daddy, I—"

"No, your father's words are wise. What Gráinne has proposed is our best—and it seems our only—option," Donal agreed, his own words well considered as he tried to make sense of it all. He turned to face Grace: "When do we leave?"

"Tomorrow morning. It wouldn't be practical for us to set off tonight. Nobody is ready, and the darkness will descend much too quickly." Grace wasn't sure how she knew when they should depart—she'd never even been sailing before—but she agreed with herself as the words left her mouth. It seemed to make sense, regardless of how her thoughts had come about.

"I'll round up the men this evening to let them know. What do you propose I tell them?"

"I think it would be best if you just let them know that we will be setting off for England tomorrow. I'll hold a meeting at eight o'clock in the morning to inform them what is to happen."

"I could cook breakfast before we set off!" exclaimed

Cathleen.

"As lovely as the breakfast sounds," Donal said, "you can't possibly come with us, Cathleen."

"Donal, please let me!" She slumped back into her chair.

"It's not right for girls to be out at sea."

"But Miss Gráinne's—"

"Gráinne's different. We need her to steer the ship. Besides, what would your father think?" He turned to Mr O'Flynn, hoping for support.

"Cathleen is sixteen now, Donal. She must learn to take responsibility for her own actions. If she wishes to risk her life at sea, then this is something I shall have to deal with."

Mr O'Flynn's attitude toward his daughter was unexpected, and Grace quite liked his surprisingly modern approach.

"Gráinne?"

"If Cathleen wishes to join us, then she shall."

It wasn't what Donal had hoped to hear. He knew that Cathleen's life would be in danger, but he had to accept his sister's wishes. She was, after all, the captain.

"Thank you, Miss Gráinne!" Cathleen leapt up and ran round to the other side of the table. She dropped to her knees and threw her arms around Grace. "I've always wanted to sail on your ship. I'm ever so grateful!"

Grace placed a hand on Cathleen's back. She wasn't sure if she'd made the right decision or not in allowing such a young girl to join them, but it didn't seem fair that she was denied the opportunity to travel with them just because of her sex. It was likely that she would soon be facing betrothal, and this may be her only chance to experience the sea.

"You're welcome, Cathleen. If you would all please excuse me, I think I'd like to go for a walk so I can go over the plans for tomorrow and make sure everything is in order."

She must have been walking for over an hour by the time she reached the highest point on the hill. Cathleen had offered to take the letter to Mrs O'Coyne's house as she was sure that her son would be able to send it on and ensure that it reached Black Tom. With the departure for England taken care of, Grace was free to go over the next stage of the plan.

In all the time it took her to walk up the hill, she had struggled to formulate a solid strategy. She had to confess, if only to herself, that she didn't really know what she was doing. She was surprised that she'd not actually revealed her true identity yet, or that the others hadn't realised that she wasn't actually Captain Gráinne O'Malley. She certainly had no idea what she was going to do tomorrow, but she hoped something would come to her soon. If it didn't, Tibbott would remain in captivity.

She reached the peak of the hill and planted her feet firmly on the ground, her posture straight. She hadn't set off with the intention of climbing the largest hill on Clare Island, but her feet took her there without explanation. Croaghmore stood at over fifteen hundred feet tall, and offered Grace a view of the island that took her breath away. It was hard to make anything out, with the mainland situated over five miles away, and the harbour almost as far, but around her stood a wonder so sublime. Perhaps this was once the land of her ancestors. She had never thought to trace her roots. She knew only one side of her family had lived in Belfast throughout the previous century. Where their predecessors, and the other side of her family, originated she couldn't say. Maybe they had been frequenters of Connacht. It couldn't be ruled out that their blood had been dispersed across the border, her past linked more closely with the spot on which she now stood than she was aware of. She glanced down at the earth. And it was only then that she truly noticed the conditions of the land. It was undeniably vast and visually appealing, but what Donal had been saying earlier about failing crops and the diminishing of the land—the result of the thieving Lord Bingham—was becoming very clear to her. She crouched closer to the ground and ran her hands over the grass. Up close it wasn't as luscious as it looked when viewed from a distance. She knew in her heart that it had once thrived, but now it felt coarse and frail.

"It's as if the land is dying," she muttered to herself.

Straightening up, she faced the sea on the west coast. The waves splashed as the wind picked up, the chill growing bitter as the night drew in.

"Tomorrow we sail for England," Grace addressed the sea, "and I will lead the voyage. I do not know how or why this has happened, but I do know that it must be done. Allow us a safe journey, and if you are able to, I ask that you guide me. I feel lost, and confused, and I cannot be sure that I've made the right decision."

She was no longer talking to the sea. Whether or not she was doing so consciously, she had begun to address Gráinne, hoping that somehow she was out there listening to her.

"There is nothing left to do but hope for the best. My life is at risk, I understand that, but you have entrusted me with this duty, even if it is for reasons beyond my understanding."

The wind picked up, blowing Grace's skirt around at her ankles and causing her loose hair to dance behind her. She locked eyes on the water, fixing her attention on one spot. Soon she would have to descend the hill and rest. And then the plan would come to her. It would have to.

"I will not let you down, Gráinne." There was no tone to her voice, the wind spreading her words across the water. "No matter what happens, I promise I *will* rescue Tibbott. Your son will return home soon!"

16

*T*he morning was unusually silent as Grace paced along the grassy bank. Behind her the *Pirate Queen* stood waiting to be boarded. It seemed to tower over her much more than she had remembered. Everybody thought she was the captain of this ship, but Grace Byrne didn't know the first thing about going to sea.

Nor did she know how to address the large crew of which she was supposed to be in charge. Donal approached from a distance, followed closely by a huddle of men. They were all dressed in similar attire and they all sported the mid-length beard that Grace had begun to admire. These men were labourers, skilled and strong.

Grace's eyes widened as she tried to count the men. There must have been thirty marching toward her. She was sure there would be no men left on the island once they had left for England, and that thought was enough to make her feel nauseous.

"Gráinne!" Donal shouted as he waved in her direction. She returned the gesture weakly, the smile on her face artificial, unlike that on Donal's, who was a natural-born seaman.

He bounded up to her and embraced her in a hug. For a moment, Grace's worry lifted as she allowed her thoughts to wander to Andy. She had grown used to Donal looking almost identical to him, but there was the odd occasion when she struggled to view them as two completely different people. Certain qualities—the fact that Andy would sometimes become vacant to the entire room when he was fully focused on the task at hand, for example—were shared by both.

"Are we all set then?" Donal was grinning excitedly as he thought about the voyage ahead.

"Nearly so."

The men assembled in a cluster in front of Grace and Donal. She knew they were waiting for her to deliver the plan.

"I'm afraid this is all we can manage, Captain." a scruffy looking man with a rip in his left sleeve spoke at the front of the huddle.

Grace shuddered when she heard the word 'captain', knowing how much everybody was counting on her. She had to make this work.

"Michael's right, Gráinne. Numbers aren't as great as they used to be. Some of our strongest men have started to weaken from the poor health conditions, and there's no way they'd be fit to cope with this journey. It wouldn't be fair to ask them to do so. Still, I'm sure we will be able to manage."

Grace wondered just how large a crew Donal was suggesting Gráinne O'Malley had once captained. Her admiration for the female pirate increased; how she managed to order so many people—so many *men*—Grace could only imagine.

"We won't let you down though, Captain Granuaile!" another man piped up.

"I know you won't," Grace responded. She thought about that name: *Granuaile*. It was spoken with such a mark of respect. A respect which, Grace had to admit to herself, she had always longed to receive. She had started to give up hope of gaining any recognition for her hard work and dedication at the Anchor office. And she felt a bit guilty for indulging in this new respect. It was a respect that she knew was not rightly or wholly hers, but as she considered this she also found herself glancing down at the boots on her feet: Gráinne's boots! They no longer felt alien to her. In fact, now that she considered the situation, she had become rather comfortable with her surroundings. For the first time, she felt like she was ready to take on the responsibility that had terrified her for months. She inhaled deeply, absorbing the air of the sea as she prepared herself to say goodbye to Grace Byrne and welcome on board Gráinne O'Malley.

You can do this, a voice inside her head told her. *I know you can.*

She listened. She knew in her heart that the voice was right.

"Listen up!" she projected. "This morning we are going to sail to England, and once there we are going to rescue Tibbott!"

A few of the older men cheered and whooped.

"Yes, yes, you may be excited. This is certainly going to be a fateful journey. However, we must not forget that my son has been captured, as I am sure you have all heard by now, by one of Queen Elizabeth's men." She started pacing in front of the crowd. "It's true that Tibbott attempted to overthrow those who try to rule over us, an act which I am certain many of us would love to emulate. But Tibbott had not considered the possible outcome of his approach. Consequently Lord Bingham—"

The men booed and hissed at the sound of his name.

"—took his opportunity to seize my son and lock him away to prevent any further threat to Her Majesty's kingdom. Tibbott has already spent time in Limerick Gaol, and it will not do anybody any good if he is to remain in England for the same duration, if not longer. Together we will make our way to London, and once we are there I will ensure that I am able to speak with the Queen herself. I know that it may sound unlikely, or even impossible, but it is our only hope."

There was silence for a moment as they absorbed the plan, until one man spoke up: "What will you say to her?" Michael asked.

"You need not be concerned; all will be prepared before our arrival."

It astonished Grace to find that she actually believed every word she was saying. She wasn't sure where her words were coming from, but she knew she spoke the truth.

She pulled out a map from inside the long sleeve of her chemise and bent down toward the sand. She'd found the map inside Gráinne's writing desk when she'd returned to the castle the previous night. She was sure the map hadn't been there earlier when she had discovered the writing paper, but she had finally come to accept that she should expect the unexpected. More than anything else, she was just thankful that it was there, as it had made planning the journey a lot easier than it otherwise might have been.

Cartography was not Grace's forté. In fact, she barely knew how to read a map. She found that when she was looking at this one, however, it made a lot more sense to her than it normally might have made. She assumed that this had something to do with Gráinne, and she appreciated whatever knowledge was being provided to her.

The crew moved closer and lowered their backs so they could get a better view of the map. This wasn't the first map they'd seen, so what Grace was about to say would probably make more sense to them than it did to her.

"We need to sail south into St George's Channel, and then continue down to Land's End. From there we'll sail up the English Channel, through the Strait of Dover, until we reach the estuary of the Thames. After that, we face our biggest challenge. We must sail up the River Thames and finally anchor in London"—a few men in the crowd growled and spat at the mention of the city—"where we will gather ourselves for Tibbott's rescue."

The men took in the information. The fact that nobody had any questions was a good sign to Grace, as they must at least have accepted the route they were to take, but she could still see some looks of uncertainty across their faces.

"Gentlemen," she commanded, "you may board!"

On his cue, the men stormed toward the vessel and began clambering up the wooden plank and onto the ship.

"Captain Gráinne," Michael said as he stopped in front of Grace. "I wish you—all of us—the best of luck on this journey." He took her hand in both of his. "I served your father for many years, and now I will remain as loyal to you as I was to him. Whatever we encounter, I promise to remain by your side. I remember the day that young Tibbott was born as if it were yesterday. I could see the love in your eyes for him then, just as I do now. We will bring your son home to you. You have my word."

"Thank you, Michael," Grace replied. "I know that your words are sincere." She watched as he wiped a tear from his eye with the back of his hand and joined the rest of the crew on board the ship.

Once the last of the men had boarded, Donal and Grace turned their attention to each other. "I hope this works," Grace said. "I don't even want to think about what will happen if it doesn't."

"Don.t give it your time or attention, Gráinne. You know what you are doing. The crew all trust you. *I* trust you. Everything will be fine. Once you have worked out what you're going to say to—"

"Hey! *Granuaile*!"

Before Donal could finish his sentence, he was interrupted by a large man storming toward them. Two figures marched on either side of him, but they were much smaller in height that he was and they seemed to be in less of a hurry as they scuttled along to keep up with his strides.

"What does he want?" Donal sighed.

"Princess, I'm talking to you!" The man directed a long, high-pitched wolf-whistle at Grace.

"You wait here, I'll sort him out." Donal put his arm in front of Grace as he moved forward. "He must have heard about Tibbott."

The man reached them and came to a halt, the two others standing behind him at either side to form a stumpy triangle. Standing in front of Donal, their clothes appeared neater, and less worn than his. Their hair was shorter too, tidier, and their beards had been trimmed so that they didn't look as unkempt. With the exception of a single gold band around one of Joyce's fingers, they were free of decoration or any sign of great wealth, but they were otherwise well groomed.

"What do you want, Joyce?"

"Absolutely nothing, Donal, my good man," Joyce claimed, patting a hand on Donal's shoulder and forcing him out of the way. "I'm just here to see the lovely Gráinne."

There was a sinister look flickering in Joyce's eyes as Grace came face to face with him. She was shocked to find that she didn't feel uncomfortable around this man as she had expected, but instead she had become annoyed, agitated even. There was something about him that suggested to Grace that he was nothing but trouble, and she didn't particularly wish to engage him if she could help it.

"What do you want?" she growled.

"As I told Donal, little princess, nothing at all; but news of your little plan has travelled downwind to Galway, and I just thought I should let you know that I think you're wasting your time. The quicker you realise that your precious son will be stuck over there forever, the sooner you can give up with this stupid plan and stop with the silly games. They'll probably have killed him before you arrive anyway!"

Grace wanted to hurl herself at Joyce, but Donal, having anticipated her actions, held her back to prevent her from worsening the situation. The two men standing at either side of Joyce broke their silence, chuckling. A snarl crept across Joyce's mouth.

"Where would the little princess be without her big brother to help her out? How sweet it is of him to stop you from doing anything you'd regret."

"Leave off, Joyce!" Donal snapped, taking another step forward and jabbing a finger into Joyce's chest. He towered above all three of them.

"Don't worry, Donal." Joyce took hold of his finger with his whole hand and eased it away. "We'll soon be leaving. I wouldn't want to be stuck on this island anyway. I mean what I say though," he said as he started walking backward. "Why don't you just leave the men to do the men's work, and you can get back to your safe little domestic life and look after the children? Goodbye, Princess!" He waved as he turned and headed off in the direction he'd come from, his mute friends following obediently. His howls of laughter could still be heard as they clambered out of sight.

"I swear, if he called me 'Princess' one more time, I was going to punch him." She tried to slow her breathing as she calmed herself. What right did he have to go around projecting his vile misogyny at her?

"Don't listen to him, Gráinne. You're the best captain I've ever known. The things you've seen and done over the years—I bet Joyce wouldn't have a clue! He's just jealous of you because he can barely steer a ship in the right direction. And we *will* rescue Tibbott, you know we will."

"Yes, Donal. I know." Grace wasn't sure she meant that, but it was all she could say as her eyes were locked in the direction where Joyce and his merry men had disappeared, his words racing through her mind. He had spoken with bitterness and hatred, but at the end of the day, what if Joyce was right?

Everybody was in place. The men had scattered across the ship, checking this and sorting that as they prepared to set sail. Grace made her way around the deck. She hoped that they thought she was just ensuring that their roles were being fulfilled and that everything was in working order, but in reality she was trying to organise the different areas of her ship in her mind before they left. If nothing else, moving around helped to steady her nerves.

"Nearly ready, Captain!" Michael announced as he hastily removed a knot from the mainsail.

"Thank you, I am glad that everything is in order."

Grace continued to walk the deck until she approached the stern of the ship. Cathleen came bursting out of the doors to the crew's cabin. Unfortunately, she hadn't been lucky enough to escape the evils of Joyce, as she'd come bounding down the hill toward the ship shortly after Joyce had left, swinging what looked to Grace like a picnic hamper from her arm. "Who's that man?" she'd asked after she'd walked by him, but Donal decided it wasn't worth a proper response.

"Nobody with whom you need to concern yourself, Cathleen," he replied, hoping the young girl would never have to be on the receiving end of Joyce's bitterness.

A grin spread across Cathleen's face from ear to ear. "Miss Gráinne!" she beamed as she took in the breadth of the ship.

"Cathleen, would you be kind enough to inform the men that we are ready to leave?"

"Oh, yes! Absolutely!" Accepting her responsibility, Cathleen bounced back through the doors of the cabin and out of sight.

Grace turned to face the ladders that led to the captain's cabin. She knew it was there that she belonged. She'd had no difficulty in racing back up the ladders when she'd rushed to return home on her first visit to the island, but now she had a duty to fulfil, and the thought of taking that next step was daunting.

She placed a hand on a rung just above her head and pulled herself up. She ascended slowly, taking each step one at a time with caution. The ladder was longer than she had recalled. Eventually she reached the top. She straightened herself and looked around.

There it was, right in front of the door to her cabin: the steering wheel.

She inched toward it until she was standing right behind it. Her eyes moved forward so she could take in the entire ship. It looked larger than before, as she watched the crew return to their positions on deck. The two smaller masts were ready. It was just the mainsail that they were waiting for now.

Michael stood beneath it. Grace caught his eye and he signalled to confirm that all was ready. As she nodded toward him in response, he began pulling a rope. Grace watched in awe as the sail moved higher up the mast. It began to unfurl, ready to play with the wind.

Once it was finally in position Grace noticed that this sail was not plain like the other two. Instead, there was a crest spread across its background. It took Grace a second to notice that this was the same crest that had appeared in the wax on the back of the letter she had addressed to Elizabeth I. As it flapped gently in the wind though, Grace noticed something different about this version. Beneath the crest were three words: *Terra Marique Potens*.

The phrase seemed familiar. Grace was sure she'd seen it somewhere before. She sifted through her mind as she tried to retrieve its meaning. After a few moments of staring at the crest, she remembered it.

"The clan motto!" she gasped to herself. She'd read it somewhere online during one of her research sessions. It took her a moment to remember the translation, her knowledge of Latin being little to none. She whispered to herself when it came back to her: "*Mighty by land and sea.*"

She thought about the phrase. There could be no motto more significant for Gráinne O'Malley than that. From what she'd read - *and from what she felt in the boots of Gráinne*—there was no doubt that it was a perfect motto.

And she knew this sentiment was one she was bound to follow. On this day the motto was not only for Gráinne, it was now time for Grace Byrne to rise to the challenge and live up to Gráinne's O'Malley's name.

Donal gave her a wave from the deck, a signal that it was time. Grace inhaled, then shouted with as much gusto as she could summon, "Up with the anchor!"

From somewhere down below she heard the anchor being hoisted as several men obeyed the command. This was it. The moment had finally arrived. There was nothing left for Grace to do except steer the ship out of port. She moved her hands over the wheel, trying to steady the tremors in her fingers. From the crafted wooden wheel stretched six handles, each one reaching out from the centre of the circle, and Grace stretched out her arms at either side to measure it. Her arms barely exceeded its width, her own frame standing tiny in comparison. Her left hand reached for ten o'clock, and her right hand for two, and her fingers grasped the wooden handles.

"Off we go, boys! London's calling!" Her shouts were greeted with a chorus of cheers from below as she turned the wheel. She laughed joyously as the *Pirate Queen* slipped away from the shore. Grace no longer felt as if she were playing a part; she had become Gráinne O'Malley.

17

Lord Bingham scurried along the corridor, clutching the letter tightly in his fist. How proud Her Majesty would be of him when he delivered it to her. Once she found out who it was from he was bound to be rewarded. Even Her Majesty could not deny that he had assisted in bringing her to him.

He stopped outside the room. The door was closed, but he knew she was in inside. Voices drifted from within. He pressed his ear against the door to listen.

"Your Majesty, there is not much time left. Something must be done with the boy to prevent questions being asked, and—"

"Do you not trust my judgement, my Lord?"

"Yes, Your Majesty, of course I do, but—"

"Then we shall leave it at that. I shall ensure that young Tibbott will come to no harm until we are ready to proceed with a full execution. And I can assure you, Lord Burghley, that it will be most satisfying. As long as we are able to bring the mother here, I see no flaw in my plan. She must not feel that she is in a position of power. Now, will that be everything for today?" she asked.

"Yes, Your Majesty."

He bowed and started for the door. Bingham shuffled out of the way just in time to save him from being sent flying into the room. Lord Burghley had left and the door was closed again, but instead of knocking he decided to remain hidden behind it for a moment. If he'd just heard the muffled sounds correctly, then Her Majesty was not going to receive this letter well at all. If it looked like Gráinne O'Malley was the one coordinating their correspondence, then she would not be happy. Perhaps it would be best if he just quietly walked away and carefully disposed of the letter. If she never knew it had existed...

The door opened.

"Lord Bingham?" Elizabeth stood in the doorway. "Whatever are you doing lurking out here?"

"Your Majesty..." he quivered. Straightening his back from the hunch he'd fallen into, he tried to compose himself. The letter was still in his hand. "There has been a note for you, Your Majesty."

"Then let me see it." She had to snatch the letter away from him as he firmed his grip on it.

She tore at the seal in one swift motion and unfolded the parchment. Her eyes flicked over the letter as she read it. After she finished reading she remained still. This had not been part of her plan.

"Your Majesty?"

"Silence!"

Bingham took a step backward at the outcry.

"This will never do! She must not interfere like this. I specifically ordered you to capture her and bring her to me. I do not recall having requested for her to come to me willingly." She thought for a moment. "Unless... Yes! Let her arrive; and I shall speak with her. She will regret the day she ever stepped foot in my palace. There is not much time until she arrives. I must prepare! Get out!"

Bingham raised a hand to speak.

"I said, GET OUT!"

He scampered back down the corridor and out of sight. Elizabeth would welcome this female pirate into the palace and there she could gain complete leverage. It seemed like the perfect plan. She didn't know why she hadn't thought it until now. With both mother and son in her grasp nothing could stop her. She turned and hurried through the door to start the preparations. There was not a second to spare. She could almost taste the satisfaction as she commenced plotting for the meeting. Revenge was sweet and it would soon be hers.

18

The voyage so far had been fairly pleasant. It had taken Grace much less time than she had imagined to learn to control the wheel, becoming used to its weight and the speed at which it turned almost instantly once they'd set sail. From her perch Grace could see that everything seemed to be going smoothly on deck too.

"Cathleen!" she called to the girl, who was standing just beneath Grace at the entrance to the crew's cabin. "Please come up here!"

Cathleen raced up the ladder and a second later was standing beside her.

"Cathleen, I want you to do something for me. I want to go down to the deck to see how everybody's getting along, but I don't want to leave the wheel unattended. Would you take the wheel for a while and keep an eye on the horizon for me?"

"Miss Gráinne, I'd feel honoured. I wish to have a ship of my own one day, something as wonderful as yours, I do hope. How I love it up here!"

Grace moved to the ladder and began the descent. 'The sea is calm at the moment so you shouldn't need to correct our heading. Just shout down to me if you need anything."

As Cathleen bounced in front of the wheel, Grace reached the bottom rung of the ladder and jumped off, landing with both boots on deck.

"Captain!" Michael called from mid-ship. He was standing tall as he adjusted ropes near the mainsail.

"All is well. Everything is working according to plan. Thank you for all your help." Grace tried her best to sound authoritative but only succeeded in maintaining a friendly tone. She liked her crew, and she thought it was important that they shouldn't think they were working *for* her, but rather that they were working *with* her. The last thing she wanted was to end up sounding like Mr Barrie.

She made her way to the starboard side of the ship where a cluster of men were gathered at the prow. She sauntered toward them, her ears now recognising the sound that was coming from their direction. She followed the notes of a woodwind instrument as she approached.

"Got this in France a few years back, I did," said the man holding the instrument. He had stopped playing as his captain stepped in front of them, choosing instead to point the flageolet in Grace's direction for her to inspect.

Grace had never seen the instrument before and couldn't remember ever hearing its name, but it resembled the recorder she used to play when she was in primary school, with a series of small holes running down the tube from the mouthpiece. The sounds it made were certainly very similar. It brought back memories of the hours she'd spent in the music room after school, the chaos of cellos and violins and recorders all squeaking and screeching at once.

"I'm just having a walk around the deck," she said, smiling at the man with the flageolet.

"Cearney's been giving us a merry song to keep us going, Captain," said one who was sitting on top of a crate.

"And Breandan's been bashing about on that old crate like a lunatic. Fancies himself as a bit of musician, so he does." Another sneered at Breandan cheerfully as the cluster of men mocked and chuckled.

"Leave off, I was just having fun." Breandan blushed.

They were only teasing him, but Grace could tell Breandan was taking it to heart. "Well, I thought your addition of percussion alongside Cearney's playing was very..." she hesitated as she thought of the right word ..."effective! Yes, it added dimension to the music."

"See, the captain liked it!"

"Yes. Well, I'd better be off."

Grace headed back up the deck before there was a chance to be sucked further into the conversation. Cearney started playing his flageolet again as Breandan returned to drumming on the wooden crates. Grace smiled as she noticed the other men dancing out of the corner of her eye.

"Thank you, Cathleen. I appreciate your help," said Grace as she climbed the ladders.

"I'm always happy to help you, Miss Gráinne. I've enjoyed being up here. The view is splendid!" If she wasn't careful, her smile would soon tickle her ears.

Satisfied that everything below was in working order, Grace took her position at the helm. She turned her attention to the mainsail, admiring the beauty of the crest.

As she was observing the design, an unexpected drop of rain fell onto her shoulder. It was hard, wet. She glanced up at the clouds above to meet the blue-black sky that was moving in from the west. This was the last thing she needed.

"Gráinne!"

Grace panicked when she heard Donal shout. There was a force in his voice, an undeniable fear. She glanced round, frantically searching for him. She finally locked eyes on him as he waved to her from the top castle.

"Gráinne! Over there!" He was pointing at something now, something behind Grace. She swung round and hurried to the side of the ship.

She gasped.

Another heavy drop of rain landed at her feet as she turned her attention to the telescope on the upper deck. She drew the eyepiece toward her and peered through so she could see it as closely as Donal was able to. It was even worse than she had first thought.

The ship was heading straight for them. Grace had feared a run-in with another vessel as it would throw them off track, an upset to her plan which she knew they couldn't afford. There was no time for mishaps or alterations; Tibbott's life was at risk and they had to act fast. It hadn't even occurred to Grace that they might be confronted by evil pirates.

She stared at the black flag waving menacingly from the other ship. The skull seemed to glare at her as it brandished swords in the place of crossbones. She shifted the telescope so she could read the name that was carved onto the side of the ship:

Devil's Orifice.

"That can't be good," Grace uttered to herself.

"What is it, Miss Gráinne? What's wrong?"

Grace jumped up. Cathleen was by her side now, with her shawl pulled over her head to protect her hair from the increasing downpour.

"Cathleen, I need you to run down to the deck and inform everybody that it is almost certain that we're about to be attacked." Her heart was racing, the words shaking as they left her mouth. She could hardly believe what she was saying.

"Oh my!" Cathleen gasped. "Yes, Miss Gráinne. Right away!" She flung herself down the steps and began racing around, informing one man then the next of the imminent danger.

Grace fought through the rain as she pushed on the wheel, turning it to try to steer away from the oncoming vessel. She knew Donal was still keeping watch from the top castle. He'd alert her when it drew closer.

Below the happy tune of the flageolet had been replaced with raised voices of men barking threats into the wind.

Grace had struggled with the wheel in her attempt to alter the ship's course, but it was too late.

Now she could see it closing in on them. The wind seemed to favour the other ship, the oncoming storm driving it closer and closer.

"Gráinne, what's the plan?" Donal called to her once he'd climbed down onto the deck.

"We fight! Ttell Michael to prepare the cannon. We haven't much time."

"Right away!"

"Cathleen," she called down to the girl, who was looking particularly lost as she tried to shelter in front of the cabin, "I need you up here again."

She scrambled up the ladder, her heart racing as she climbed. There was no way she was going to let her captain down.

"Miss Gráinne! What are we going to?"

"Stay calm, Cathleen. I need you to take the wheel again. I need to go inside for a moment to get something, but I want you to come for me if you see anything through the telescope. I should just about have enough time. I won't be long."

Before Cathleen had a chance to respond, Grace had disappeared into her cabin. She didn't know what had made her think of it, but she knew that it was finally time to bring it out.

She'd panicked the first time she'd seen it, she couldn't deny that. It had seemed threatening. Now, however, she had never been more thankful for anything in all her life. She lifted the lid up from the chest, praying it was still there.

It was.

Lying on the bottom of the wooden chest was the sword that had frightened Grace on her first visit. It stretched across the full length of the chest, the thin blade gently curving to narrowly miss scraping against the side panel. She reached for the handle, clasped her hand around it.

She leaned forward as the ship rocked, Michael having just fired the cannon. Grace prayed it had reached its target.

She steadied herself and pulled out the sword. There was a striking beauty to the weapon that she could not deny. The silver blade gleamed, as if brand new, not four hundred years old, as the candlelight reflected off its surface. The handle moulded around Grace's hand as the metal curved into a protective dome. It was patterned with a line of rubies running round its centre. Each one glistened, the colour of blood.

Grace stumbled as the entire ship rattled with the collision. The front of the *Devil's Orifice* had bashed into the Irish ship, causing it to shudder under the pressure. The cannon had missed its target. They were now under attack.

Grace's hand tingled as she brandished the sword tightly, preparing herself to face the fight. It was heavier than she had imagined, but not unmanageable. She charged out of the cabin and through the doors, clutching onto it. She wasn't as nervous to brandish the weapon as she had expected, but instead she was filled with a sudden sense of satisfaction that came with holding it. She leapt off the upper deck, not giving a thought to the ladders, and landed with a thud on the deck, both boots firmly on the surface.

Just in time.

The crew watched as the captain of the enemy ship swung onto the *Pirate Queen*. He was clutching onto his own sword, just as Grace had anticipated. This only reassured her that her thoughts had been accurate: this was not going to be an easy battle.

The captain of the other ship sauntered toward Grace's

crew. They had now all assembled, holding out all manner of swords and cutlasses in the direction of the oncoming attack. It struck Grace as odd that there was nobody behind this other captain. Nobody had followed him off the ship. There was no way he would be able to take on everybody standing before him on his own.

He was quite short, only slightly taller than Grace, and had hair almost as long. His heavy black curls cascaded neatly down the sides of his face, his dark beard thick and tidy. His moustache was slightly curled at the sides, twitching as he snarled, his lip curving up toward his pointed nose. A broad hat rested on top of his mass of curls, its crimson colour complimenting the healthy tints in his cheeks.

His coat was ruffled red velvet, reaching down to his knees and fastened with shiny gold buttons. His cotton breaches were a clean white, tucked inside his smooth and untarnished black boots. The single gold earring in his left ear reflected the weak light.

"Well, well. What do we have here?" he said as he took a step closer to the crew.

He spoke with an affected English accent.

"Who are you?" Donal demanded, his teeth gritted as he brandished his own sword in the direction of the pirate.

"Who am *I*? Dear boy, surely you must know who I am! I am the great Captain Bellingham!"

Captain Bellingham's bellow was met with silence.

"Sorry, *Bellingham*," Grace said, stepping to Donal's side at the front of the huddle, "I'm afraid we've never heard of you. Now if you'd be so kind as to get off my ship—"

"Your ship?" Bellingham roared. "How amusing! Surely the most entertaining thing I've heard in a long time."

"Captain Gráinne O'Malley is the finest pirate I've ever known, and you'll be sorry you ever stepped foot on her ship!" Michael shouted, not entirely sure whether or not it was something he would soon regret.

"Is that so?"

Cheers came from the crew standing behind Grace.

"Well then, perhaps you would allow me the opportunity to prove you wrong. Men!" He barked the last word, and on cue a rush of pirates came tumbling over the *Devil's Orifice* and onto the *Pirate Queen*. The crew, only slightly smaller in number than Grace's, appeared to be of a lesser wealth than Captain Bellingham, which was made clear by the quality of their attire, but they were still clothed in finer garments than Grace's men. As they assembled they looked like the traditional pirates in the children's stories Grace had become familiar with in her youth. If she started to hear the sound of a ticking clock, she knew they'd all have to flee.

Captain Bellingham lunged at Michael, his sword drawn. Michael and Cearney took up the battle with Bellingham as Grace came face to face with a filthy looking pirate. His eyebrows were dark and bushy, his hair long and ragged. He grinned at Grace, showing off several blackened teeth.

Grace flashed her sword, the metal of the blade clanking against that of her foe. All around the ship the battle was waged. Suddenly, a high-pitched scream sliced through the air. All heads turned toward the upper deck. Grace gasped as her eyes locked upon the rogue who was tugging at Cathleen. She was gripping firmly onto the wooden barrier in front of the wheel, but she could feel her hand slipping. She wasn't going to be able to resist much longer. The sharp point of the pirate's sword edged closer, threatening her throat.

And then her hand slipped.

Before anybody was able to move, the pirate holding onto Cathleen leapt, swinging his arm around her waist at the same time, and jumped from the upper deck directly onto the *Devil's Orifice*. Had the vessel been another inch away from the other he wouldn't have made the jump, and he and Cathleen would have fallen into the ocean. Instead, they stood alone on the deck of the ship, Cathleen locked in his grip with his sword millimetres away from her throat. The pirate gritted his teeth and forced a breathy laugh as everybody stared at him.

"Walsh!" cried Bellingham. It was clear by the look on his face that this was not what they'd intended. They had wanted gold, jewels maybe. But not this...

His beady eyes locked on Cathleen. He found himself licking his lips as he studied her. Perhaps Walsh had done well after all. Without warning he charged back onto his own ship, hungry for his reward.

His crew followed him back onto the *Devil's Orifice*. Everyone on Grace's ship was too stunned to move. They had to do something. Cathleen's screams grew louder as the ship was being set for departure.

They couldn't leave without her. But if they all crossed onto the enemy ship it would leave them exposed and vulnerable, and possibly without a vessel if they didn't think of something quickly. They could all be seriously injured, or even killed, and there would be no hope left for Tibbott.

Donal couldn't stand it any longer. He knew he should have waited for his captain's order, but there a pain shot through his heart with every cry that Cathleen uttered. He refused to let them hurt her.

"Go!" Grace shouted to all her men a split second after Donal had moved. They obeyed and leapt across to the other ship, which was met with great uproar as they landed in several huddles. Grace, the last one on the *Pirate Queen*, inhaled to steady herself as she took a few steps back.

One wrong move and Cathleen could be killed. They were all now in more serious danger than they ever had imagined. Regardless of whether or not instructing everybody to invade the *Devil's Orifice* was the best response to the situation, Grace knew that it had to be done. She was also aware that the fight about to commence was going to be telling.

She ran toward the edge of the ship and jumped.

19

*T*he battle broke out immediately once they'd landed on the deck of the *Devil's Orifice*. Lashing out with their weapons against their adversaries, Gráinne and her crew hoped to strike whomever they could, and the only sound to be heard was the metallic colliding of swords.

Donal had charged with such haste and such force that he'd caught Bellingham's leg with his sword, slightly south of where he'd intended to strike him, but the pain was enough to cause Bellingham to fall backward from the wheel. He maintained his grip on Cathleen however, as he clutched tightly onto her arm.

"Leave her alone!" Donal shouted.

"Or you'll do what?" Bellingham mocked.

"Or you'll answer to me!"

"Miss Gráinne!" Cathleen called.

Grace arrived with her sword brandished in one hand, her other hand poised to steady herself. She knew Bellingham was not going to back down. Grace lunged at her foe. Bellingham forgot that he was holding onto Cathleen and brought his own sword forward as they began their volley. Donal wasted no time in pulling his sister away. As Grace and Bellingham began to battle, he moved her to a safer place.

Then he shifted his attention back to what was happening on the deck. Donal knew where he was heading. He had no time to waste.

Thunder rumbled in the distance as he sliced his sword through the rain, aiming for Bellingham's side. But he misjudged the distance, missing Bellingham entirely. However, he *did* hit Bellingham's sword, the weapon flying out of his hand and across the deck. Without it, he was unarmed and unable to fight.

This was Grace's chance. Her heart raced as she stared into Bellingham's eyes.

"Why don't you just step aside?" Bellingham offered Grace, as if it were kind of him to call an end to the fight. There was an obvious panic in his voice that he was unable to hide.

"Not a chance, Captain." She wasn't prepared to let him go.

"Then perhaps you will at least allow me to get down on my hands and knees to say one last prayer..." He moved slowly toward the deck, his eyes fixed on his sword.

Donal leaned forward and grabbed his collar, pulling him back to his feet as Cathleen grabbed Bellingham's sword and pointed it at him.

Grace knew that this was her chance. The sword felt weightless and natural in her hand. She lunged forward, as if a force previously unknown to her was directing her every movement.

And then she stopped.

Bellingham was panting now, his eyes full of the unknown. With their captain kneeling on the ground, his crew stared in disbelief. Grace held firmly onto her sword, then lowered it and turned away from the fallen pirate. She made her way to the edge, ready to cross back over to the *Pirate Queen*. "We shall not be defeated!" she shouted, and a cheer was raised by her crew.

Once all were accounted for and back on board the *Pirate Queen*, Grace made for the helm. A few of her own men were bleeding, and one had taken a nasty gash to the face, which he was currently trying to clean with rain water. Most important though, was that they were all still able to continue with the journey.

Donal joined her on the bridge as the sound of Cearney's flageolet eased the tension of the bygone battle. The melody this time was not gay but mournful, and there was no chatter or merry singing; everyone was weakened and weary. After a time, Cathleen joined the captain and her brother in the wheelhouse. "Miss Gráinne ," she asked, "why did you spare Captain Bellingham? Certainly, he did not deserve your mercy!" Grace stared out to sea, both hands resting on the wheel. "Courage does not reside in the sword, Cathleen, but in the knowledge of knowing when to use it."

They had triumphed over the *Devil's Orifice*, but there was a force much more powerful that they still had to reach before they would be able to save Tibbott.

They still had to face Queen Elizabeth.

20

To everybody's relief, the rest of the journey went much more smoothly. The rain continued to splatter down onto the ship but by the time they were approaching their destination the wind had calmed and the sun had eventually started to peek out from between the clouds. The crew took this as a positive omen, but Grace wasn't so sure. She had guided the ship toward the estuary of the River Thames, and now there was no going back. This was it. They had arrived in England.

The river appeared much narrower now than she had remembered. Admiring it from the pier next to the London Eye as she had done many times during the summer months with university friends, it looked vast, enormous. But trying to steer a ship up it and navigating through its twists and turns made it feel uncomfortably small.

As they moved slowly upriver, the crew all turned to gaze around them as they took in the view. None of the younger ones had ever seen London before so the sights were interesting, if not what they had expected. To Grace, however, it was all bizarre.

This was not the London she knew. It wasn't anything like the London in which she had spent the last nine years of her life.

"It's so *big*!" exclaimed Cathleen, who had taken to standing by Grace's side at the wheel. "Look at all the buildings!"

Grace didn't respond. She couldn't. The frequent complaints about living conditions back home in the twenty-first century were often justifiable, Grace had often thought, but looking around her now, she realised things could be much worse.

She hadn't really thought about what London would look like four hundred years in the past. She had been so focused on her pending encounter with Queen Elizabeth I that her mind was filled with all sorts of imaginary conversations. Now that her attention was on her surroundings, however, she fought with her emotions as she struggled to comprehend the fact that she was so much closer to her current home than she had been in a long time, and yet she couldn't be any further away.

As they continued along, the soot that filled the air around them was undeniable. The buildings were much smaller than Grace would have expected, most of them crumbling or falling apart, their window panes hanging loose, their doors cracked and broken. The further they moved up the river, more and more people seemed to line the streets; even from a distance Grace could tell that it was unlikely that any of them had much money. Their clothes were frayed, filthy and worn.

She tried to divert her attention as they approached their final destination. She wished she had been more prepared for the arrival, but she hadn't been able to concentrate on anything other than what it was she was going to say to the Queen.

She'd taken advantage of the calmer weather conditions once they were making their way to Land's End to work out what she was going to say. She wasn't sure if any of it would work, and she couldn't be certain she'd even be able to remember anything once she was standing in front of the Queen. She had to keep reminding herself that there wasn't any guarantee that she would see the Queen. There had been no way of knowing whether or not the letter had been received.

"If only I could have sent an email," Grace mumbled to herself.

"What did you say, Miss Gráinne?"

"Nothing, Cathleen. I was just going over my plea."

The ship passed a large building that stood with much more grandeur than the others. Grace was too busy looking directly ahead to notice it, having forced herself to stay focused on guiding them safely along the final stretch of the journey. For this reason she did not see the woman staring down at them from a window high up in the building.

Elizabeth grinned as she watched the *Pirate Queen* sail past her. Soon she would be able to complete the set— mother and son—and at last she could quell this threat to her empire. The orders had been sent out already. Now it was only a matter of awaiting the arrival of this female pirate at her palace. She smirked, pleased that everything was working according to plan, and stepped away from the window as the ship moved out of sight.

"You're going to be fantastic, Miss Gráinne. And you're so brave!" Cathleen declared.

Grace didn't respond as she steered the ship toward the wharf near London Bridge. The bridge looked nothing like it did in Grace's time, built from stone instead of the concrete and steel she was accustomed to seeing.

The ship finally docked as the crew stared out at the land, awaiting their orders. Donal climbed the ladder to the upper deck and put an arm around Grace. "We've made it, Gráinne. I knew you could do it!"

And Donal was right. The year was 1593, and the *Pirate Queen* had arrived in London.

They walked up the uneven road toward Thames Street, with Cathleen a step behind Donal and Grace as she eagerly took in her surroundings. Grace had ordered the crew to stay on the ship, preferably in their cabins out of sight, so it was just the three of them dealing with the situation at hand.

"But what if we become bored?" Michael had protested.

"Well, I can see there's plenty of ale around," Grace responded, gesturing toward the back of the cabin.

"Now that's more like it!" cheered Breandan.

"And I know some of you are brilliant at storytelling. I expect you'll be able to have quite a fine time while we're away."

"But—"

"Michael, I am sure you will understand that it is much safer for you to stay here. You must remember that there is no guarantee that the Queen will have even received our letter. Whether or not she is willing to accept my request is not yet something we are able to know. It would cause great alarm if we all took off and marched through the streets of London. I'm sure that that would not go down well."

"Right you are, Captain," Michael finally admitted.

"And if anything should happen to us while we are away—"

"You mustn't speak like that!" A few of the men mumbled something about how they were going to be just fine and assured them that they didn't need to worry. Grace hoped that they were right, and could tell by the pained look on Cathleen's face that she'd frightened the girl, but it was something that had to be said. Precautions needed to be taken, just in case.

"*If* anything should happen to us, then I'd like you, Michael, to take charge and captain the ship back to Clare Island."

"Yes, Captain." He stood up and saluted her, before sitting back down. "It would be an honour."

"Right then, gentlemen," she continued, "let us be off. When we return, we will have Tibbott with us!"

They left the cabin to the sound of cheers, knowing too well that it was the last positive thing they were likely to hear for a while. Grace tried not to concentrate on the fact that it might be the last positive thing she'd *ever* hear.

"Is anybody else hungry?" asked Cathleen as they continued up the road.

"I'm sure there will be time for us to eat something soon, Cathleen." Donal realised that perhaps Cathleen, whose mind seemed to easily wander, hadn't quite realised the severity of the situation into which they were about to enter. But how could she? He had to remind himself that she'd never been away from the Clare Island before.

Grace didn't respond to either of them. The mention of food had started to make her feel queasy, the atmosphere around her turning her stomach.

It would have been normal to see ships docked next to the bridge, Grace realised, and it was likely that most arrivals came with some sort of wealth. It made sense that beggars occupied these streets. Up close she could see that their faces were lined with dirt, the germs spread thick across their faces and hands and feet—feet, she noticed, which were often bare or poorly supported.

A woman was sitting in a doorway, her brown hair loose and scruffy around her face, with an old blanket wrapped round her shoulders. She hugged a grubby bundle. The soft cries of a starving baby could be heard drifting out of the old cloth. A man reached out his hand as he pleaded to the three new arrivals for some food. Grace shook her head at him. It broke her heart, but there was nothing she could do. She'd seen homeless people many times before in her own century, but these conditions she found hard to fathom.

Donal drew her closer to him to move her out of the

way of the beggars. "I don't understand why it's so disgraceful here. They're taking everything from us, Gráinne, but it doesn't seem to be doing anything positive for anybody."

Grace couldn't help feeling guilty as she took a step further from them. She was about to utter an apology to the man whose begging she'd had to reject when they heard a voice from the top of the road.

"You three! Come here!"

The man had been watching them, standing up ahead at the point where the short road met what Grace would have referred to as Tooley Street. He made no signal to them but continued to stare as they approached.

Grace assessed his appearance as they drew nearer. He was tall and thin, and well dressed in a rich burgundy cloak. His face looked wooden, his nose narrow and long and pointed.

"Gráinne O'Malley, I assume. *Captain* Gráinne O'Malley" He scoffed as he spoke her name and title.

"Then my letter has been received," she presumed.

"If you are referring to the letter in which you requested an audience with Her Majesty Queen Elizabeth, then yes, it has been received. I would not be standing here waiting for you otherwise, would I? My name is Lord Burghley, Mistress O'Malley. I have been sent as Her Majesty's Lord Treasurer to bring you to her. We expected you would be arriving soon, and so transportation has been arranged for you presently."

"You mean—"

"Her Majesty will see you, Mistress O'Malley. In fact, I dare say that she is looking forward to the meeting. However, this does not mean that she is in favour of your request. It merely indicates that she wishes to issue her command to you in person." He gestured toward Donal and Cathleen. "Who might I ask are these two?"

"This is my brother Donal, and our dear friend Cathleen, Lord Burghley," Grace said. "They have accompanied me here from Clare Island."

"Well, you better bring them with you. We cannot have them roaming the streets. Follow me."

Grace was relieved that Lord Burghley hadn't expected other members of her crew. She had been right to instruct them to stay inside the cabins. They were at least out of danger there.

The carriage was not a small rickety affair like most of the contraptions that bumped their way along the streets. Next to the mule carts that carried produce or coal for fires, it appeared to be from a different world entirely. It was larger and much grander than the others, black in colour and finished with delicate detailing on the metalwork. After all, it *was* the property of Her Majesty.

The three heaved themselves onto the step at the side of the carriage and clambered inside. "Does the Queen sit in here?" Cathleen whispered to Grace, who was sitting opposite her. "Don't be stupid, girl," Lord Burghley scolded as he slid in next to Cathleen, "Her Majesty has her own carriage suitable only for Her Majesty. This one is used simply to collect those with whom Her Majesty wishes to speak."

The coachman whipped the horse into action upon Lord Burghley's command, and the carriage began to make its way along the road.

After a long journey in silence they finally reached the entrance to Greenwich Palace. The horse and carriage continued up the pathway toward the main entrance of the building. It slowed to a halt and the coachman climbed down from his seat to open the door. Lord Burghley was the first to exit. The other three waited until he had given them permission to alight.

The main entrance to the palace consisted of two large doors, each made from dark wood with a thick iron handle. A man stood at the side of the door. He was dressed similarly to Lord Burghley, but his clothes were a little more threadbare, made from a lesser material. He kept his eyes forward, not looking at the arrivals.

Lord Burghley stood at the front as he faced Grace, Donal, and Cathleen, who were standing in a line. "You must not, under any circumstances, speak to Her Majesty unless she has specifically requested for you to do so." The tone in his voice suggested he quite clearly assumed they were uncultured creatures who had been taught neither manners nor morals. "You must not touch anything, and you must remain beside me at all times while we make our way through the grounds. I do not know why Her Majesty is so keen to accept your request, and you might be glad to hear that she has instructed me specifically to not tie your hands"—Cathleen gulped, her face turning paler—"but I am not to argue with her decisions. Now if you would please follow me..."

He turned and headed for the doors, which were opened swiftly by the man who was positioned at the entrance.

The entrance hall was vast, polished and gleaming. The ceiling was high, causing their footsteps to echo as they made their way deeper into the building.

They continued along several corridors. Aside from a few family portraits that lined the walls, there wasn't much to see. Grace assumed Lord Burghley had taken them along a route which would allow them to see as little as possible of the Queen's private palace. Eventually they stopped outside another door, this one narrow and not as tall as the one at the main entrance.

"It will do you well to remember everything I have told you," said Lord Burghley. He knocked lightly on the door.

Somebody on the other side turned the handle and the door as it opened. Grace inhaled and held her breath as she waited for the room to be revealed to her. She exhaled as quietly as possible, preparing herself for the moment she'd been waiting for.

With the door now fully open for them to enter, it was time to meet Her Majesty Queen Elizabeth.

The room was relatively dark, so they were able to see very little as Lord Burghley led them inside, each one walking in single file with Grace in front, and Cathleen following Donal. A narrow crimson rug ran the length of the room, protecting the royal floor beneath it from unworthy feet. Grace looked down at the shape of her boots as they walked across the carpeted surface. She thought about how Gráinne would have made the exact same steps. She wondered how she had felt when she knew she was approaching the Queen. Grace's heart beat wildly in her chest. She had no idea what to expect.

As they reached the top of the room it began to grow brighter. This end was illuminated by candles, with the lower end kept in darkness to prevent visitors from absorbing too much of their surroundings. Once at the bottom of the rug, Lord Burghley stood still in front of Elizabeth. The others stood directly behind him, unable to see her.

"Your Majesty," he bowed as he spoke, "Captain Gráinne O'Malley and her associates." Cathleen and Donal noticed his etiquette and followed his lead, but Grace found herself rooted to the spot where she stood, her hands shaking. After receiving a nod from Elizabeth, Lord Burghley made his way to the side of the room.

Donal and Cathleen edged to one side of Grace so that Elizabeth could see them, but Grace remained several metres away from Elizabeth yet directly in front of her.

Grace gulped as she looked into Elizabeth's piercing eyes. No matter how unprepared she felt, whatever happened next was something she knew she was going to have to face. There was no going back now.

"Mistress O'Malley," Elizabeth said in an affected politeness, "allow me to welcome you to my palace. How kind of you to visit!"

21

That's...Elizabeth I?!

Elizabeth's image wasn't far removed from some of the more iconic portraits that had been painted of her, but now that Grace was standing right in front of the Queen she could see, quite distinctly, that her facial features were similar to—no, *exactly like*—Fran's. The likeness seemed almost impossible.

"Mistress O'Malley!"

Before Grace could consider the resemblance any further, Elizabeth spoke to her, her voice high in pitch. Grace didn't respond, remembering what Lord Burghley had said to her outside. It didn't seem like a question.

"I expect you are wondering why I was so willing to see you today," Elizabeth continued. It was rather peculiar for Grace to find that Elizabeth was speaking to her in Latin. What was more bizarre was the fact that Grace understood every word that she was saying. It had become apparent that language barriers did not take effect on this side of reality. "You will understand that I do not allow anybody into my palace without good reason. However, upon receiving your letter, I found it to be most interesting. You see, Mistress O'Malley,"—Grace expected such a use of her name was no more a sign of friendship than it was a gesture of courtesy—"it is rather unusual for a female like yourself to be in such a peculiar position, and to be so proud of it of as well! And you are from Connacht, is that correct?"

"Yes, Your Majesty," Grace managed to respond.

Elizabeth leaned over to whisper something in the ear of the guard who had been standing next to her. He was average in height with a length of blonde hair by his neck. His face was motionless, void of all expression.

As Grace nervously watched Elizabeth speak to the guard, she noticed a faint tickle on her arm. She reached up to discreetly scratch at the area, but as she touched her chemise she noticed that there was something *inside* her sleeve. As cautiously as she could she edged it down. She didn't need to remove the object all the way before she noticed her name at the top of the parchment.

It was unmistakably the same letter she had found inside Gráinne's boot when she had first discovered the portal at the top of her stairs. Without having to fully remove the letter to read it, its words began filling her with their support and courage.

"Right away, Your Majesty."

Grace's attention snapped back as the guard spoke. She watched him bow and exit the room, and took advantage of the opportunity to stuff her letter firmly back up her sleeve and out of sight.

Elizabeth turned to her again: "It cannot be denied that your courage is admirable, Mistress O'Malley. It is not every day that somebody can stand in front of me, dressed as you are, and neither kneel nor show any sign of remorse. So often I must look down on pleading, pitiful faces. Your unusual confidence is almost a welcomed change."

Grace was fairly certain she didn't feel confident, but she was pleased that she was managing to appear so.

Perhaps this admission was all she needed to summon her strength.

The guard returned almost immediately and held open the side door. Another man appeared with his back turned as he pushed Tibbott inside. Grace was unable to see his face as he walked with his body turned away from her. Tibbott, however, she could see quite clearly.

James?!

"Tibbott!" Cathleen screamed.

"Silence!" Elizabeth cried out, stunning Cathleen. The poor girl was shaking as she huddled closer to Donal. He tried to calm her but his own eyes were ablaze with fury at the sight of his nephew chained in front of him.

It was not the sight of her surrogate son that had disturbed Grace, but the fact that, as far as she could see, it was James standing before her. His bright blonde hair was unmistakable, even though it was now dirty and matted, and his watery blue eyes were identical.

Tibbott was pushed to the corner of the room, his hands and feet remaining tied together as the man who had brought him in fiddled with the chains to ensure he could not escape. The young boy looked up at his mother, but he knew better than to speak to her. Grace could feel her own eyes watering as she looked at the broken, fragile boy, so close yet so far away from her.

"Thank you, Lord Bingham," Elizabeth said to the man standing beside Tibbott.

Grace's sorrow quickly changed to anger when she heard the name spoken that she knew had brought so much turmoil to Irish soil. Her blood began to boil as he tightened Tibbott's chains.

Her anger quickly changed again to confusion when Lord Bingham finally turned around. Grace had thought she had come to accept the situation, but seeing her boss standing right in front of her as he held tightly onto the iron chain that was connected to the boy she recognised as her fresh-faced colleague, altered that. Lord Bingham appeared to be the double of Mr Barrie, with the same bitter smirk spread over his face.

But there was no time for contemplating how any of this could be possible as Elizabeth demanded her attention.

"Now, Mistress O'Malley," she pressed her hands onto either side of her throne and lifted herself, "please move a step closer."

Grace obeyed, taking a step forward.

"Thank you." Her words were soft, not at all as threatening as Grace had first perceived. Elizabeth also stepped forward, leaving behind the support of her bronze high-backed throne, and poised herself.

"Mistress O'Malley, I expect you think that you are in ownership of the sea..."

'I have earned the respect I am shown in Connacht, Your Majesty. I would never *expect* anything. It is a trait most unflattering." Grace heard the words as they left her mouth. She couldn't deny that she had spoken them, but they were not her own.

"I know I have the body of a weak and feeble woman," Elizabeth began, "but I have the heart and stomach of a king. Do you think that I am not able to see right through you? You have been a traitor to England for many years. This meeting has been long awaited, I can assure you."

"I do nnot deny that, Your Majesty."

"You appear overly proud of this identity you have fashioned for yourself. It is hardly conceivable!" She threw back her head and laughed loudly. Lords Bingham and Burghley joined in her mirth.

"Hush!" she ordered them to silence. They obeyed immediately, straightening up to reassert their positions.

"Dear boy Tibbott," Elizabeth continued without looking at him, "I do not know how you are able to remain upright when your mother partakes in such a filthy, masculine activity as piracy. If I were you, I would most certainly find myself crippled with shame."

Tibbott lifted his head for a chance to exchange a glance with Gráinne, but as soon as Bingham detected his movement he slammed his hand onto the back of his head, forcing his eyes back down to the ground.

"Lord Bingham, there will be no need for that. Please, allow the child to look at his mother. It is the least we can allow him. After all, if it was not for him, I would not have the pleasure of inviting Mistress O'Malley here today, would I?' Her eyes widened into a sinister glare.

Grace looked at Tibbott for a moment before he returned his attention to the floor. He knew better than to take advantage of what was offered to him so reluctantly. He knew Bingham would punish him for it later, but it was worth it just to look upon the woman who had raised him, the mother he knew he had let down. He would never be able to forgive himself if any harm came to her in England.

Elizabeth's voice heightened in both pitch and pace as the conversation snapped to the treason of her prisoner. "Your son, Mistress O'Malley, has been a mischievous little boy. Fortunately for me, Lord Bingham—a loyal servant to me—put a stop to your son's miscreant behaviour. Locking him up was but a simple precaution to ensure that he was in no position to further seek the destruction of my empire."

Tibbott's head remained bowed but Grace was certain she could see him wincing as Lord Bingham tugged at the chains to tighten them, snarling as he moved.

"So you are here to request that I set your son free," Elizabeth continued. "However, I do not believe that it would be a wise decision. My throne is much safer while this Irish brute is locked away. Wouldn't you agree, my Lords?" She didn't turn to face Lords Bingham and Burghley as they agreed with her in unison. Instead she kept her eyes locked firmly upon Grace.

Grace, in turn, did not look away from Elizabeth. She was transfixed by her wig of rich red hair, large enough to hide a thousand secrets, and the giant skirt of her dress which must have made it nearly impossible for her to walk.

Elizabeth was silent now. Grace took this as her cue to speak. She swallowed to clear her throat, straightened her posture in preparation for addressing Queen Elizabeth I. "Your Majesty, Tibbott's actions may be reprehensible, but I have come here today to offer an explanation for the behaviour of my clan, and that of the people of Ireland. We are continuously looked down upon, repeatedly spat at and gibed. That much we can endure. Such insults do not affect our ability to survive. However, it is the undermining of our physical conditions which have made it nearly impossible for us to live harmoniously.

"Perhaps the extent of our suffering has not been fully revealed to you, Your Majesty. The force with which we are punished for merely existing is stronger than that with which we are able to cope. We try to stand up, but repeatedly we are pushed to the ground, and that ground we fall onto is diminishing. The reason for Tibbott's revolt was a consequence of further land reduction on the west coast. Lord Bingham has seized another plot, which was being used to grow crops to feed our people. Every time one of your subjects helps himself to our land, we are forced to face further hunger.

"Your men do not pay for what they take, and so we do not have the means of exchanging with other landowners. We are quickly running out of land sufficient for growing food. We have but a few patches of malnourished grass, which must be kept for the cattle to graze. Our animals are weakening as rapidly as our crops are failing. People are becoming ill, and many of them are dying because they do not have the strength to recover.

"Mothers have become too weak to feed their babies, children too fragile to grow and develop. Our men have little strength left to bring in enough fish to sustain our population. I am here today to request that you consider not the way in which my son has behaved, but the reasons why he felt he needed to respond the way that he did. In our time of desperation, we depend on the arrival of change, and this change is something only you can command, Your Majesty."

Grace bit into her lip nervously. Elizabeth remained silent. Grace could feel everybody's eyes upon her. Lords Bingham and Burghley glared at her. Donal and Cathleen, who had remained as motionless as possible, looked at her with hope, Cathleen's eyes streaming with tears. Tibbott had lifted his head just enough so that he was able to look at his mother. He prayed silently that the Queen would find no derision in what had been said. If she did, then the consequences would be dire.

"Mistress O'Malley," Elizabeth finally said, "you speak to me in a manner I find fascinating. It is unusual for one to address me so boldly. If nothing else, I admire your approach."

"Your Majesty, if I may," Lord Bingham interrupted.

"I am not finished, Lord Bingham," she snapped before returning her attention to Grace. "However, I still struggle to see exactly why I should allow your son to go free. How can I be sure that he will not repeat his despicable actions? After what you have done against my people, I must wonder why I should not lock you up with your wretched son and throw away the key!"

Cathleen gasped.

"Your Majesty, I shall not be restrained. I will not hide who I am."

"So many have died at your hands—"

"That has often been beyond my control."

The room returned to silence as Elizabeth paused to think about what had been said. She concentrated on Grace, focusing her attention on her eyes.

At that moment it was as if there was nobody else in the room. A sadness in Elizabeth's eyes reflected in the eyes of Gráinne O'Malley, nad in the eyes of Grace Byrne. In that moment they looked at each other not as opposing figures of authority, but as two women living in a world where they were continuously challenged. The pain of Elizabeth's own suffering was silent but unmistakable, and it was not hatred and venom that looked back at Grace, but understanding and empathy.

"Perhaps we can come to some sort of understanding. An agreement," Elizabeth finally said. "I will allow young Tibbott to return to Ireland—"

"Yes!" Cathleen was unable to refrain from squealing. Donal held onto her to stop her from running toward Tibbott, who had to force himself to keep looking at the floor. A look of horror had spread across Lord Bingham's face.

"Quiet, please! Allow me to finish. Mistress O'Malley, I shall allow your son to return to Ireland, and Lord Bingham will return to you the land he has most recently confiscated." Grace was sure Bingham was about to weep. "However, I must ask in return that you do something for me." Her request could be absolutely anything, and Grace knew it. "I ask only that you never return to England. This rule also applies to the men under your command, and to anybody with whom you find yourself acquainted. I will cooperate with your request on the condition that you do the same with mine. If I am ever informed of your presence near English soil again, I will have your entire clan put to death. Do we have an agreement?"

Grace considered the offer. She quickly realised that she had to accept it.

"Your Majesty, your proposal is one to which I am happy to agree."

Elizabeth smiled. "Good. Well then, Lord Bingham," she continued to look at Grace as she addressed him, "Release the prisoner!"

There were tears in Bingham's eyes as he began to unchain Tibbott. Elizabeth remained standing in front of her visitors, her lips pressed tightly together. It was a moment Grace knew she would never forget. Never had she imagined she'd be standing in a room with this striking monarch. Her power was undeniable, but her beauty was eternal.

No final words were exchanged between Grace and Elizabeth. Nothing more needed to be said. Between them a recognition had been sealed, an understanding that neither could have predicted. There was just enough time before Grace was led away for Elizabeth to lower her head in a subtle nod. As Grace caught the gesture she bowed, a mark of her own newfound respect for the woman with whom she had presumed to have nothing in common. How wrong she had been! In their final moment together, both women looked at one another and smiled ever so subtly.

22

Standing at the bottom of the hill, Andy stuffed his hands into the pockets of his coat to keep them warm. He looked unusually casual in jeans, with a scarf wrapped around his neck. He must have only been standing there for two minutes, and yet it felt like a lifetime had passed.

Paranoia had started to take hold of him. What if he'd gone to the wrong stop? Perhaps he'd written the time incorrectly. There was still another ten minutes until she was due to arrive, but he couldn't help but fret that he'd messed up somewhere. He had no idea why he was so nervous. There was nothing to worry about, he knew that. It was just that he liked her—really liked her, in fact—and had never felt as happy as he did when he was around her. If his plan was going to work, he needed everything to go just right.

He blew air into his hands and rubbed them together, cursing himself for forgetting his gloves. Had December been this cold last year? Things would warm up when she arrived though—they would be able to start walking to keep the chill off them...

As he turned he saw her. There she was, right on time,

heading up the road toward him. She looked radiant, even as the wind reddened the surface of her cheeks. Her hair was tied up, he noticed—a wise decision in this weather. He had always liked the way she wore her hair. It accentuated the features of her face.

"Hello, stranger," she said once she reached him. Her greeting was awkward. She knew it as soon as the words had left her mouth. Was she blushing? She hoped she wasn't.

"Miss Byrne!" he responded just as awkwardly. What was wrong with them? Why were they both so nervous? "Shall we?"

They entered Hampstead Heath, both walking with their hands clamped in their pockets.

"I'm glad you agreed to walk with me tonight." The area was almost deserted as they had made their way among the trees.

"You are?"

"I've been stuck inside the house all day and desperately needed to get a breath of fresh air," he said. "I swear I was close to going crazy."

"I know how you feel. This is one of my favourite spots to go walking. I can't say I've been to many places as beautiful as this, if any."

"I'm ashamed to say I've never been up here before." They turned the corner and stopped by the lake.

Standing in silence, they admired the way the trees were reflected on the surface of the water. A coot glided along the water, creating a trail of soft ripples behind it.

"The flowers are quite remarkable, aren't they?" Andy commented.

"Which is your favourite?"

"Definitely the blue ones... I couldn't tell you what they're called, of course, but they're very pretty."

Grace grinned. "Do you want to see something even prettier?"

"Even prettier than all this..." Andy tried not to make

his flirting obvious, wondering whether Grace knew he
was referring to her as much as he was to the Heath.

"Yep."

They walked in silence, side by side, as they continued
along through the trees, making their way up the hill.
"Here we are!" Grace announced once they'd reached the
top.

They stood at the viewpoint as they stared out across
London.

"So, what do we have here?" Andy glanced at the
information board in front of them that featured a long
line of buildings to help with the identification of
London's skyline. "Ah yes, the Gherkin. Unmistakable,
isn't it? And that over there looks to be the Shard," he said,
pointing to a thin building in the distance. "Some of the
architecture is wonderful, isn't it?"

"I've always loved the look of St Paul's Cathedral,"
Grace added. "It's such a wonderful shape, and the colour
of the roof is beautiful."

"Where is it from here?"

"If you squint you can see it," she edged closer to him
so that her body was slightly pressed against his, "right
over there." She pointed to the area where it could be seen.

"I think I see it!" Andy turned to face her as he spoke,
his eyes catching hers. They faced each other for a
moment before Andy uttered a low cough from the back
of his throat, awkwardly shifting his attention back to the
view.

Grace took in the panorama of London, transfixed by
its vastness. Forever expanding in every direction, there
were patches of greenery juxtaposed with industrial chaos.
London really was wondrous.

But as she stared in silence the scene started to shift in
her mind. The large buildings were replaced with squat
single-story structures. Everything turned dark as the air
thickened with the haze of coal fires. No longer was her
attention in her own time; it had returned to her other

reality.

Everything had been so clear in her mind when she'd awoken that morning. The agreement with the Queen had been sealed, and Lord Burghley had escorted them in the carriage back to Thames Street, Tibbott included. He'd watched as they lifted anchor and retreated toward the English Channel, leaving the city behind them.

The crew had managed to stay below deck just as their captain had instructed. It had been Michael's idea, Grace later learned, for them to tell each other stories about their travels, and that had kept them occupied. Everybody was safe. They were all going back home.

The journey back to Clare Island had been safe but slow, and by the time they had reached the halfway point, everybody had been so drained of energy that it was decided that they would take turns being on lookout for invading ships.

Grace had slipped off her saffron dress and her leather boots and slid into bed, eager to rest. The last thing she remembered hearing was Cathleen calling through the door: "Goodnight, Miss Gráinne!"

"Goodnight, Cathleen," she had muttered. She'd closed her eyes and fallen into a deep sleep.

When she awoke in her own room in her own home she felt profoundly disappointed. She sprang out of bed and made for the door at the top of the stairs, but she couldn't see it. She banged on the wall and called out, but it was no use. It was gone.

She made herself a cup of tea and sat down at her desk, unable to stop her mind from running over the previous night's events. At least she assumed it had only been one night; she was struggling to keep up as time had started to blur into one existence. With nothing else to do, she opened her laptop and typed everything she could remember: the dangerous encounter with the *Devil's Orifice*; the look of desperation from the homeless woman as she clutched onto her starving child; the venom in Lord

Bingham's eyes; and the unexpected empathy in Queen Elizabeth's.

It took her a long time to realise that she was not writing in third person as she made her notes, but was instead constructing them in first person. It now seemed almost bizarre for her to consider herself to be anybody other than Gráinne O'Malley. She had become so used to the identity that there was no longer anything unnatural about it to her. To leave her behind seemed almost unthinkable.

She continued tapping away, her mind flooded with images of Donal and Cathleen and Tibbott. She could still hear the squawks of the gulls and the lapping of the sea. Beneath her hands she was sure she could still feel the pressing of the ship's wheel as she grasped it. It had all happened so many centuries ago, and yet for Grace it was fresh in her mind.

It was only when Andy had texted her to ask if she'd like to accompany him on a walk that she was able to drag herself back into the twenty-first century. The one part of her mind that had allowed itself to remain as Grace Byrne couldn't refuse his offer. She replied to his message, suggesting they visit Hampstead Heath, and shut down her laptop while saving her notes to be continued later.

She'd managed to keep Gráinne O'Malley off her mind for the entire afternoon, with both her heart and her attention firmly fixed on Andy. However, as she looked out across London now with the sun setting in the sky, her mind and heart raced as everything she had locked away several hours ago instantly came flooding back to her in a surge of overwhelming emotion.

A tear trickled down her cheek.

Andy must have seen the tear out of the corner of his eye, as he turned to face Grace. He couldn't possibly understand why she was crying, Grace was sure of that, but she didn't question it as she watched him lift his hand toward her face to wipe her cheek with his index finger.

He held it there for a moment before he cupped her other cheek with his right hand. He didn't speak as he leaned towards her, but pressed his lips against hers.

Grace had never known a sensation so magical: as Andy held onto her back, his body pressed firmly against her own, she felt like she was being kissed for the very first time. The more he kissed her, the more she felt herself floating on air. She was a free spirit soaring through the sky without worry or care. Their connection had made the moment something special that belonged only to them.

23

*"H*ow can you possibly prefer cricket to football?"

"We played a lot of it at school. Don't get me wrong, I love football. How could I not?" Andy removed his coat and slid it onto the back of his chair. The conversation had started ten minutes ago when he arrived to find that James was the only other person in the office. James had asked Andy what he was up to that day, and he'd mentioned cricket. James had practically fallen off his seat.

"Fair enough; but I still don't see how you can prefer any sport to football. Football's the greatest thing in the world!"

The door clicked shut as Grace came bustling in, her handbag wedged underneath her arm as she tried to balance the box she was struggling to carry. She dropped them both onto her desk. Andy left James to muse over his football teams and started for Grace's side of the room.

"Hungry this morning, Grace?" He nodded toward the large box of doughnuts that was now on top of a pile of loose papers.

"Oh, those?" she responded, flustered after her battle with the combination of vicious wind and the climb up the staircase to the office. "They're not for me." She unbuttoned and removed her coat, dropping her gloves into her bag. She reached in and pulled out an A4 plastic folder. "Is Mr Barrie in yet?"

The office door opened.

"Don't be so stupid, Moira. Of course I haven't got time to do that. No, you'll have to pick the kids up from their club. No, I've just told you. I haven't got time... Goodbye, Moira." He jabbed at his phone with a thick finger to end the call.

"I think he might have just arrived," Andy replied after the whirlwind had headed into his own office, Fran following him as she clutched onto two cups of takeaway coffee.

"Well, that's good. Because in here," she held up the folder, "is the finished article."

"You've done it? Fantastic! Can I read it?"

"I'd rather you didn't. Not yet, anyway. I'm really nervous about it as it is. I have no idea what he's going to think."

"And you went with the pirate thing in the end?"

"I stuck with the pirate thing, yeah."

"Well, I'm sure he's going to love it. I know that may seem like a bit of a stretch for Mr Barrie, but you're a good writer. He'll be able to see that."

"I hope you're right, Andy."

"I know I'm right." He placed his hand on her arm. She didn't flinch at the touch. He was smiling at her, his body turned away so that James couldn't see his face.

"I had fun the other night. Thank you," he said softly.

"So did I," she said as she smiled back. She was relieved that Andy wasn't able to read her thoughts, as she couldn't help picturing him from the Sunday morning. He'd emerged out of her bathroom after his shower with only a towel wrapped round his waist, his hair messy and water dripping onto his torso. The image was now ingrained in Grace's mind, and she didn't intend to remove it.

He hadn't been able to stay long in the morning as he was due to attend some sports event—Grace didn't really ask many questions about it—but he was there long enough for them to share jam on toast for breakfast. It was a silly thing to be amused by, Grace knew it, but for so long she'd fantasised about that sort of thing, and about Andy, that she still couldn't quite believe any of it had happened.

"It's not like me at all, you know. I don't usually jump into bed with...well, you know." He blushed, trying to ignore the sound of his own voice.

"No, Andy, neither do I." She too was blushing now. And yet, she didn't seem to mind.

"It's just that I...how do I say this? You're very...Grace, I like you." He spoke a little too loudly, snapping his head round to make sure that James hadn't heard. Luckily he'd already put his headphones in to zone out for the morning. "I really like you. I was kind of hoping we could do it again sometime."

"Andy—"

"Not just the sex," he said, catching himself. "All of it."

"Andy, I'd love to."

Grace had never seen such an excited grin on another person. It was definitely the answer he'd been hoping for.

"Well...good! I'm glad. I better get started with some work as it's a day of tight deadlines for me, I'm afraid. Do come over and let me know how you get on though won't you?"

"Of course I will."

He winked at her before turning his attention to his computer. The butterflies in Grace's stomach refused to escape her. They'd arrived when he first kissed her on the top of Hampstead Heath. They were still there when he started to unbutton her shirt back in her bedroom. They were definitely still there in the morning when she woke up with her arm wrapped around him, and they still showed no sign of leaving. It was all so new and exciting;

for the first time in years she had discovered a real reason to get up in the morning, something more important than her writing and career and personal success. She had found love.

Once Andy had kissed her farewell and headed off on Sunday morning, Grace had pulled all her energy together and forced herself through the article. It took her most of the day, and she was sure on several occasions that she wasn't going to get it finished, but she knew she had to power through it or she'd never get it done.

She took the article out of the plastic folder and clutched onto it. In a few seconds she would walk into Mr Barrie's office with her head held high and present her work to him. What happened after that was out of her control.

The door opened and Fran walked out. It was now or never.

Grace picked up the box of doughnuts and carried them into Mr Barrie's office, pausing outside the door. She knocked lightly against the frosted glass panel. There was no answer. Should she knock again in case he hadn't heard her?

"What is it?" came the grunt from the other side of the door.

Grace pushed open the door just enough so that she could stand in the gap between the door and its frame. "Mr Barrie, sir, I have something I'd like you to read. If you don't mind, that is..." Her nerves almost caused her to stutter.

'Well, come in then; don't just stand there. Sit!"

"Right, yes. Sorry." She tried not to sound as flustered as she felt. The last time she'd been inside Mr Barrie's private office had been her interview day. He still had the same high-backed green leather chair trimmed with metal studs. The dim lighting, a product of there being no windows in the small space, darkened the blood red carpet. There was a wooden display cabinet to the left of his desk filled with family photos and hand-made gifts from his children; Grace expected he kept them there to prevent his wife from suspecting his adulterous behaviour on the off chance that she came to the office unannounced. Not that it *would* happen—in the years Grace worked at Anchor she'd not once actually seen any of Mr Barrie's family.

"I also thought you might like these," she said as she handed him the box of doughnuts.

There was a mumble from the other side of the desk, which Grace assumed had been a thank you.

She sat down, still clutching onto the article. She was starting to lose all confidence, but she knew she must not let the boss see that if she wanted to convince him that she deserved more responsibilities than those she currently had.

"Mr Barrie, I was wondering if you'd possibly be able to read this? I'd like to know what you think of it. Your opinion would be invaluable—"

"What's it for?" he interrupted.

"Nothing specific," she managed. "It's just something I wanted to write, and I just felt that, if you liked it, then maybe...maybe you'd perhaps.."

"Spit it out, girl!" He licked a piece of strawberry icing from his moustache. "I haven't got all day."

He was right. She had to pull herself together if she was going to make a positive impression on him. This was her only chance, and she knew that all too well. She paused for breath before straightening her posture.

"Mr Barrie, sir, I'm really proud to be part of the Anchor team, but I don't really feel like I'm always given the opportunity to put my abilities to good use. It's not that I have any problem with taking phone calls or sorting through the post, but sometimes—most of the time, in fact—I wish I had a little more to *write*. I wrote this article in the hope that you'd be able to see that I *can* write, and that perhaps you'd allow me to start producing content for the website. Alongside my other responsibilities, of course," she added for good measure.

"And that's it there?" He pointed a sticky finger in the direction of the article.

"Yes, it is. It's about—"

"You don't need to tell me what it's about. If it's a good article, I'll be able to work that out for myself. I'll read it and get back to you. I wouldn't get my hopes up though, if I were you," he grumbled. "Now, please go back to work and do what I pay you to do."

Mr Barrie turned his attention back to the doughnuts. Grace rose from the chair and left the room, closing the door behind her as quietly as possible.

"How did it go?" Andy asked as Grace approached his desk.

"I'm not sure. I handed him the article. He said he'd read it. That's about it. Maybe this wasn't such a good idea."

"Of course it was a good idea! I told you, Grace, he's going to like it."

"I suppose I'd better get back to work. He's definitely not going to have confidence in me if he thinks I'm slacking off!"

Back at her desk Grace pulled up the folder of new emails and forwarded them accordingly: two for Andy; one for James; one for Fran. She had hardly slept the night before, her nerves high concerning the article. She needed to take her mind off it while she waited for Mr Barrie to read it. Observing the office around her—a little bit of people watching never hurt anybody—everyone, it seemed, was busy tapping their keyboards as they knocked out their latest stories.

Although she'd felt a strong connection with what she was writing, with the article coming from her heart as much as it came from her mind, the words had seemed almost fictitious to her, events that had happened to somebody else and not to her—events that had happened to Gráinne O'Malley. And because she had focused so intently on the quality of the article, she had unknowingly started to build a barricade between herself and the life she was writing about. Now that the article had been written, however, and Grace had gained from the experience what was intended, it was apparently time to remove that barricade to allow her time for reflection. Without warning, and with little resistance, Grace began to lose her connection with the present.

Her eyes spun to Andy, who was staring at his computer screen, deep in thought. Except it wasn't Andy. It was Donal, his hair hanging long at his shoulders, his facial hair scruffy and dark. He was no longer dressed in the grey suit and purple tie that Andy had worn that morning, but a tattered shirt soiled by manual labour.

Grace turned her attention to James, who had been bouncing his head up and down to some pop song he was listening to through his headphones, clearly procrastinating from whatever it was he was supposed to be doing. Now, however, his head hung low. He was hunched over, just as Tibbott had been when they were inside the palace at Greenwich, and the same loose clothing hung upon his body. From where she sat Grace could detect the sadness in his eyes.

Queen Elizabeth I sat across the room from her, the large cream skirt of her outfit spilling over the sides of the little office chair. Her ruff curved round her neck, Fran's own red hair resting on its surface as it spilled down from the top of her head. From the side of her face Grace could tell that she looked paler than usual, with more vibrant blush on her cheeks than even Fran would normally have worn.

The door at the far side of the room sprang open suddenly, and Grace turned her head, a sense of wonderment now guiding her movements. The past had become her present, and her head swam in a sea of confused history and identity.

A figure emerged in the doorway, short and stout with

a thick moustache.

"Bingham!" Grace muttered to herself, her eyes locked on the spot where he stood.

Between breaths, the room shuddered. The air seemed thick as gelatine as the figures froze in motion. It was only when she heard somebody calling her name that she blinked.

"Grace? Grace! Will you please come into my office?"

Mr Barrie was staring at her from where he stood in the doorway. Grace regained her focus on her usual surroundings. Lord Bingham was gone. Donal and Tibbott and Queen Elizabeth had returned to their previous forms. The room was once again the mundane Anchor office. She had left the sixteenth century behind.

She knew that it was over.

"Yes, Mr Barrie, right away." She leapt out of her seat and headed into his office as swiftly as her legs would take her.

"Well, Grace, I must admit I'm rather surprised. This wasn't at all what I had expected," he said once they were both seated.

"Mr Barrie, I know I probably shouldn't have written it. I had no business asking you to—"

"I enjoyed it."

"You—you enjoyed it?"

"I wasn't sure what to think at first, but once I got into it, I had to admit that I actually found it quite fascinating." He leaned onto his desk with his hands folded on top of the article. He wasn't exactly smiling, but it didn't matter to Grace. He'd actually said he'd enjoyed it. He'd called her article *fascinating*!

"Just to make sure I'm following it correctly, it *is* about the effects of past events on our present day opinions?"

"Yes, that's correct, sir."

"It's all very vogue these days, isn't it? All that stuff about parallel timelines and spiritual connections. Although I don't believe in any of it myself, of course, I can't deny that there's a demand for it out there. I want you to put this on the website."

His words had been sudden, not at all what Grace had expected. Perhaps she hadn't heard him correctly.

"I think you're onto something here, especially the part where you talk about history walking amongst us without us realising it. People will eat that stuff right up. Tell me though, what did you mean when you were talking about blood links?"

"Ancestry, sir; I believe that our ancestors—spiritually speaking, of course—can assist us on our present journeys. I know I can't prove it, but—"

"I don't need you to prove it, Grace. I just need you to write it. People love tracing their roots and finding out where they come from, where they believe their genes originate, that sort of thing. There's an audience for this, I know there is. I'm going to create you a profile—"

"A profile?"

"On the website, Grace. You see, I've realised that we cover everything a digital news site needs to cover: sports, beauty, current events, all of those things. But we don't have anything general, content that won't become so quickly dated. Sports news is soon taken over by some other match. Fashion pages go out of style quicker than those fake Prada boots Fran's always wearing. They're all great to have on the site, and necessary too, but if we put this sort of thing out there, it might reach a wider audience, and at a much more frequent rate. That's why I've decided I'd like you to be my writer for the new column we're going to be running. Get this—it's going to be called 'Hot Topics'. Simple but effective, wouldn't you agree?"

"Yes, I do agree. You want me to...really, sir?!" Grace couldn't believe what she was hearing. It was the first time she'd ever witnessed any sign from Mr Barrie that he actually knew what he was talking about. Perhaps he wasn't so bad at running Anchor after all, even if he was a nightmare to work for.

"Whatever the public are buying into, I want you to write about it. If they're squealing about an infestation of poisonous spiders, I want you to cover it. If they're going crazy for calorie-free cheese, you write about it. As long as it's exciting and going to draw ratings for longer than a day, then it's your responsibility. We really need content like that on the site to attract new readers. Do you think you're up to the job?"

"Absolutely sir! I won't let you down, I promise!"

Mr Barrie stood up. "Right, well I'll set up a tab for you on the site. I want one main feature a week—you can start with this one you've written here—but I want you to do follow-up posts. Go into the streets, interview people. It'll help to publicise Anchor too if you're meeting people face to face. It's about time we started branching out. In the meantime, I need you to go back to your desk and continue with whatever it was you were doing. I still need you to maintain any incoming emails because they're not going to manage themselves. I hope you're ready for an increase in workload. This is going to be a much more demanding job than what you're used to."

"Yes, Mr Barrie. I'm absolutely ready!"

"I'm counting on you not to let me down, Grace." Mr Barrie held open the office door to let Grace out. "Fran, can you come in here a moment please? I have something for you."

Fran walked around Grace as she crossed the office. Grace wasn't going to think about whatever it was Mr Barrie was giving Fran. Besides, she was fairly certain it would be *Fran* who was giving something to *Mr Barrie*. It didn't matter though. Her plan had worked. How or why she didn't know, but her article had actually worked! She had been offered a new job. She didn't have to leave Anchor after all. She couldn't stop smiling as she sat down at her desk and plugged her USB stick into the computer, ready to format the article for uploading.

As she waited for the file to open she saw Andy coming toward her, his eyes shining. "How did it go?"

"I've been given a new job!" she squealed.

She struggled to get the words out as she began to tell Andy everything, trying to process what had happened as she was relaying it. Her plan had worked, her article had succeeded. She was in love, and better still, that love was returned.

It was insane, she knew it, and it was all happening so fast. She was going to need to pace herself, try to take it all in. Something told her that this wasn't going to end any time soon, and she could not be more thankful, for she knew none of it would be possible if it weren't for Gráinne O'Malley.

24

*E*verybody on board the *Pirate Queen* had left England with smiles on their faces. More than anybody though, Gráinne couldn't quite believe they were returning safely. It hadn't been an easy journey, but she'd known from the moment they'd left Clare Island that it would not be straightforward. Now, she couldn't help but wonder if she would have committed herself to the Queen's agreement had she been able to consider it in advance.

Of course it was silly to doubt her decision; she'd always said she would do anything for her son, and she meant it. Even if it meant that somebody else decided where she was allowed to sail. And apparently it was now the case that she most certainly was *not* allowed to sail south of Ireland.

The water lapped gently against the sides of the ship as they approached Clare Island. The mid-afternoon sun had tinted the water with a warm glow, the turquoise surface pulling the *Pirate Queen* forward, guiding it to its destination.

"Home sweet home!" Donal shouted to his sister from the deck. She glanced at him and smiled, acknowledging his cry of delight.

Cathleen clutched Donal's arm as they returned to the dock. She'd done well on her first voyage, as Donal kept reminding her, and she knew she deserved to be proud of herself. When she had time to recollect everything then maybe the reality would hit her—whether or not she'd choose to sail with Gráinne again was a decision she still had to make. That is, if Gráinne would welcome her back on board. She desperately hoped that she hadn't let her down. She'd definitely had fun though, especially listening to Michael's stories of his pirate adventures that he entertained the crew with on the way home. Yes, it had been quite a journey.

Tibbott had managed to keep his spirits up as best as he could. He didn't say much though, and even now, as he stood next to Gráinne, he remained, for the most part, silent. Gráinne had her suspicions that there was something he wasn't telling her, but she decided it was too soon to force him to speak about it. What had he experienced, or what had he seen, that he was keeping quiet about? Maybe she was just being paranoid, but she couldn't quite shake the feeling that nothing was as plain-sailing as it appeared to be.

Once the ship had docked, Gráinne addressed her crew.

"Thank you all for your hard work and dedication during our journey. It has not been easy, and it certainly hasn't been safe, but we all made it home. Better still, we made it back with Tibbott, just as we promised we would." There was a cheer from the crew as they applauded the young man, who was now starting to blush. "You may now return to your families and let them know that you are safe and well."

Everybody piled out of the ship. Gráinne walked with her arm linked around her son's; they were the last to leave the ship.

"It's good to be back on Irish soil," she remarked,

taking in her surroundings as her crew dispersed. It felt like a lifetime since they'd first set sail. It always did. She turned to see Cathleen's father hugging his daughter. "Hello, Mr O'Flynn," she greeted.

"Gráinne, how glad I am to see everybody return," he said, supporting himself on Donal's shoulder. It was clear that his health was declining. "How did it go?"

"Fairly well," she replied with a smile. "We got what we went for, and that's the main thing."

"Tibbott. I'm thrilled to see you've come home safely." He shook the young man's hand.

"And it definitely is *our* soil now, isn't it?" Cathleen bounced on the end of Donal's arm as she responded to Gráinne's earlier comment.

"Yes, Cathleen," he replied. "Yes, it is."

The five of them started up the hill as they set off for their own homes. It was their land again, wasn't it? Gráinne had trusted the Queen with their agreement. There had been no questioning it. Maybe she shouldn't have let her guard down. Was she foolish for thinking that Bingham would actually return the land he'd stolen? She couldn't let her mind think about it too much. Right now, she had to focus on spending time with her son. Tibbott was her main priority now. Her family had to come first.

Not that she was giving up quite yet. Battles still had to be won, and her union with the sea was as alive as ever. She knew her relationship with England was not over yet, but there would be time to deal with that later.

The tension surrounding the agreement she had made with Queen Elizabeth would no doubt cause opinions to divide across the island, but one thing was for certain: as Gráinne O'Malley stood at the peak of the tallest hill on Clare Island that evening, her attention fixed upon the land that surrounded her, and the sky above her illuminated by moonlight, the decision was made that her story would not go unremembered. Little did she know that, four hundred years later, she would be brought forward in time to guide another woman along her own personal journey. What had so recently become the past for Gráinne would ultimately become important in shaping the future for Grace Byrne.

AUTHOR'S NOTE

*A*rtistic license is a fine thing, isn't it?

A lot of the events I've written into Celestial Land and Sea did not actually happen. I say this—they certainly occurred inside my head, but I expect they didn't happen in real life. Given the fact that there's not an enormous amount of information readily available about GrÃ¡inne O'Malley, at least in comparison to other historical figures, and specifically her contemporary Queen Elizabeth I, I took the liberty of moulding the facts I could find so that they worked with what I wanted to write. Some of the characters are based on real people, but others—Cathleen, for example—only ever existed in my own world. Until now, that is.

I'm very excited to be able to set my second novel in Hampstead. It has a gloriously rich history. It's alive with stories and adventures. When I first visited the area several years ago I knew it was exactly the sort of place I was looking for to explore a new area of spiritualism in my fiction. Hampstead offers a lot of exploration, and I certainly have no plans of abandoning it any time soon.

I must thank those whose support has guided me

through writing Celestial Land and Sea, namely David and Kelly and the team at Open Books; the family and friends who probed me with questions about the novel's development, keeping me pushing onwards; and my personal inspirations for its characters, in particular my approach to Elizabeth I. The composition of this novel is based on a foundation comprising late nights, several dead ends, and the consumption of more cups of coffee than I can ever condone, but every second for me has been an unforgettable journey I'll always treasure. Besides, I never could resist a pirate!